Blinded by ~~Love~~ Lust

Virginia Raynor

authorHOUSE®

AuthorHouse™
1663 Liberty Drive
Bloomington, IN 47403
www.authorhouse.com
Phone: 1-800-839-8640

First published by AuthorHouse   1/4/2010

ISBN: 978-1-4567-1088-0 (sc)

Printed in the United States of America

This book is printed on acid-free paper.

Certain stock imagery © Thinkstock.

Because of the dynamic nature of the Internet, any Web addresses or links contained in this book may have changed since publication and may no longer be valid. The views expressed in this work are solely those of the author and do not necessarily reflect the views of the publisher, and the publisher hereby disclaims any responsibility for them.

Dedication

This book is dedicated to everyone that is struggling with domestic violence. I would like you to know that you are not alone. I want you to know that you can be an over comer. This story is to help avoid the violence and have a plan if you are going through a similar situation. Know that someone has been in your place before, and that they have paved the way for you to avoid your situation. Most often times, women do not make it out of their situation due to the hands of their abusers. And often then not, most abusers do not see the pain that they are causing their love ones. Have trust and faith and believe that all things are possible through Christ.

Acknowledgements

First and foremost, I would like to thank God, my Lord and Saviour Jesus Christ for putting this into perspective for me. I never knew what I was put on this earth to do, but going through the test and trials for so long I thought that this is what HE would have me to do.

For the people that always told me to write a novel instead of always reading one. Thanks. Special thanks to Monika Felton for taking the time out of your busy schedule to help edit this project. You got the first copy girl and that ain't no lie. Friends forever. Alicia Mays for listening to me and helping me get my thoughts together. Thanks girl. Theresa Davis, my hair stylist for pushing me to start this project. Eric "GQ" Gooden, you are a sexy mofo. Thanks for blazing the cover for me. My baby girl, Ashley Jones, your Godmother loves you. Daddy Devine for the photography and the graphic design. You did it well, thanks for making my vision a reality. And to that special person that came into my life. You let me know what it is like to find love unconditionally, you know who you are. Much love. To the person that believed in this project and backed it financially, I am forever grateful to you. Love you more.

Also, the two special people that made me the person that I am today. That never gave up on me and was always there to encourage me to push on to live another day. And that when trials and tribulations came my way, that I could rise about it all.

May you two rest in peace, and shine your lights down on me every once in a while. Missing the both of you with every beat of my heart.

Prologue
Winter, 1996

Lawrence wrapped his strong hand around Ebony's slim neck and lifted her up off the floor with one hand. Her feet were dangling in mid air. Her eyes bulged and saliva streamed from her lips. "Don't you know I could kill you bitch! " Ebony was gasping for air, could feel consciousness slipping from her body. She had fear in her eyes because she had never seen her man react like this. The room became dark as midnight as Ebony held on to life. "Bitch I will kill your ass!" Lawrence threatened. Before she could pass out, Lawrence released his grip and stated "Don't ever do no shit like that again without my knowledge!"

Before any of this ever transpired, Ebony was just chilling at home. A quite evening with Lawrence and Shawn, their little son. They had just got finished eating dinner, when their neighbor called for Ebony to pick up a piece of mail. The neighbor had intercepted the mail so that Lawrence would not see it. When Ebony left to go next door and return, Lawrence wanted to know what it was all about. Ebony replied, "Nothing important just a piece of mail that I was looking for." Little did she know that the neighbor had already given Lawrence an insight of what it was, a credit card. Ebony never knew that this result would come about over a credit card that was in her name and not his.

As the night went on, Ebony was scared as hell. It hurt for her just to swallow anything. Lawrence had calmed down like nothing had ever happened, and as they say it is all good in the hood. After picking up Shawn to get ready for bed, Lawrence demanded to have sex. With all that was going on Ebony was scared that if she did not have sex with her husband, another choking or a beating would be sure to follow. He was ruff and continued to thrust his manhood into her dry opening as if she was a piece of trash. Lawrence seemed like he was possessed by a demonic entity at that moment. The tears escaped from her eyes as her husband was violently raping her. She never made a sound; she just let him finish handling his business. Afterwards, she just laid there and cried herself to sleep. The next day she really wanted to tell someone, but didn't have anyone to talk to because Lawrence controlled her every movement. She was not even allowed to chat with her family unless he was around to question what they had discussed.

Chapter 1

It all started back in 1992. Ebony Washington was a twenty-one year old woman in search of the great American dream (husband, kids and a house with a white picket fence). Ever since she was little, her main wish in life was to be loved. Not saying that Ebony was not loved; she was raised by her mother in a single family dwelling. She knew her father, but he was always in prison for some reason or another. She longed to find a man like her stepfather. He came into her life when she was four years old. Ebony was not a bad looking young lady. Her self esteem was up. Most of the men that she dated growing up were dogs. Ebony's mother, Vanessa would always tell her that the kind of men she dated were "no good dead beats". She wanted something more for Ebony than she had ever had. Her favorite line was "be more than me!" Those words resonated in her mind from her younger years, so Ebony was out on a quest to try and find a different type of man.

Ebony had this thing when it came to men; she only attracted drug dealers or bums. Each man that graces her presence turned out to be like her real father. Her step father, Leroy was like "the man with the plan." He provided for Vanessa and Ebony. Leroy was that father figure that every little girl dreamt of. He spent quality time with the family, and even one-on-one time with Ebony, unlike her real father, who was always in jail. Even if he wasn't, he really never had time for Ebony. He only called on her birthday, when he thought he was about to go to jail, or if he thought he was dying. She guess she always longed for her real father's affection, but knew she never would receive it. There was something about just needing and wanting that "daddy's love." Deep in her heart, she knew this factor played a major role in her life and would affect all her relationships.

Ebony made the decision to leave home at seventeen. Vanessa, her mother backed her in that decision. She needed more out of life than the drug infested streets Baltimore had to offer. She had to escape the cycle of drug/alcohol addiction, multiple pregnancies with different men or just being stuck in an ordinary job. She joined the Navy. She thought this would help her to conquer the world! During her travels around the world, she saw things that people her age could only imagine in their lifetime. Her mother was so proud.

During the next three years, Ebony traveled to Guam, Korea, Thailand, Singapore, Japan, Philippines and finally settled in Warminster, Pennsylvania. She chose Warminster, because it was only an hour from her hometown. It had been a long journey to get back to the East Coast, but she wanted to be near her family.

Before arriving back in the United States, Ebony was in the process of having a miscarriage. Once she arrived in Baltimore, her mother took her straight to the Veterans Administration Hospital. Going through that miscarriage was hard on Ebony. This was her first pregnancy and the father was still in Guam. Ebony had met Gene on her birthday at the club. After drinking up a storm and everyone was coupling off to go home, she didn't want to be alone. Ebony invited Gene back to her room. Things got hot and heavy that night. She really didn't expect to see him again, but he stuck it out with her til she was transferred to the states. He called her every now and then to check on her, but he couldn't come to the states to go through the miscarriage with her. She had to clear her mind and get herself together mentally and physically. That ordeal put her into a semi depressive state; thank God she had her mother by her side! Her mother cared for her through that trying time. Soon, it was time for Ebony to report to her new duty station.

Vanessa, Leroy, and a host of other family members all made the journey to get Ebony settled into her new place. She knew her mother thought it was a pleasure just to have her baby close. After settling in, shopping for the barracks room, and dinner, the family made their way back to Baltimore. Ebony talked to her mother nearly everyday. Being homesick and yearning to be close to her was all she had. If Ebony didn't have money to make it home, Vanessa would instruct her daughter to travel the long route, down RTE 40, and that she "had her back when she arrived." More often, Vanessa and Leroy would make trips up to visit Ebony if she couldn't come home during the weekend. She had really made her parents so proud; she had traveled to places that they had never been.

Chapter 2

Almost a year had passed being stationed in Warminster and Ebony was sick. She was the type of person that would "self medicate" first; when that didn't work, she would go to the hospital. While reporting to sick call, Ebony saw this "fine specimen of a man." She didn't know if she was ready for another let down, but had not dated for a year now. She glazed at this man; he was about six feet tall, bald and dark skinned. His body was built to perfection, all chiseled up! He was the type of man that a woman could drool over, and could give you that ultimate orgasm just by looking at him. Damn, he was fine!

Later, she ran into her next door neighbor, Kenya, which also worked at the hospital to inquire about "hooking a sista up" with "Mr. Perfection." Kenya stated that "Mr. Perfection", the man that Ebony had set her sites on had "jumped the fence." Ebony didn't know what "jumped the fence" meant, but was later explained that "Mr. Perfection" did not like women of color anymore. Instead, Kenya suggested Ebony meet a nice man she knew. She wanted to introduce Ebony to a guy named Lawrence. Kenya gave Ebony the "run down" on Lawrence; basically it was that women used him for his money. Ebony told Kenya that she was not into using men. She wanted to be in love and to have that love returned! Ebony thought "I never used a soul in my life!" She was raised to treat people the way she wanted to be treated.

Lawrence was about five nine, dark and was not handsome by any of her standards. He had a little gut, "Jeri curl juice" dripping from his head, with large lips most would refer to as "soup coolers." He was not the usual man of Ebony's taste. She figured "What did she have to lose? Every other man she had dealt with had drama or games." Anyway, it wasn't about the looks, but what was in the heart; and if he had a kind heart, then everything would turn out fine. Kenya pumped both Lawrence head and Ebony's up. She gave each person the other's phone number and said that the other person gave permission.

After the initial phone conversation, they decided that they would get to know each other a little better. Later that day, Lawrence decided that he would stop by to see Ebony. The two conversed and chatted for what seemed like hours. The plan was that when Ebony got off of medical the next day, he wanted her to come over for dinner. The invite was for a personalized home cooked meal prepared by him. She was excited because no man had ever cooked for her before!

Ebony very seldom met a man at their home on the first date. She figured that since they both were in the military, he could be a trusted shipmate. If something went down, at least she knew where he worked. His apartment was only across the street from the base and she was willing to take the chance.

For the date, she decided she would wear a tight pair of Levi button fly jeans. This was a precautionary measure just in case he tried something; it would be hard for him to get into those pants. When she arrived at his apartment, he had the candles flickering, slow jazz grooves playing and even had wine. He was doing the damn thing to impress her, showing off his culinary skills! The dinner was fantastic, he could really cook.

Afterwards, the two sat on the couch and watched a movie. Ebony didn't see what was coming next, but Lawrence was really trying to "hit that." They say you never give it up on the first date, but "damn, he had her hook, line and sinker." Lawrence had that smooth ass Barry White voice and charmed her right out of her panties. Before she knew it, she was in his room with her clothes off! The initial sex was nothing like Ebony had ever experienced in her life! Lawrence orally pleasured Ebony's body and his package was nothing but the truth! He rocked her world; she thought "those soup coolers came in handy." After the initial night of passionate sex, Ebony thought that the incident would just be a booty call. He insisted that she spend the night with him. Ebony told him that she had to go to work in the morning. He persuaded her to stay. "You have plenty of time early in the morning and still get to work", Lawrence stated.

The next morning Ebony made it to work on time. The events of the previous night played over and over in the back of her mind. It had been a long time since she had sex anyway. At least he released some "bottled up tension" that was built up inside of her. She figured once she got home after work, she would chill and get some rest. That didn't happen; when she arrived home, she checked her answering machine and Lawrence's voice was on the other end. Ebony didn't know what to think of the situation. He was cool, but she just didn't want the night to turn out as a disaster. Little did she know that before she went to work each day, there would be a call from him. At the end of the work day, he either wanted her at his place for dinner or they would go out to eat. Two weeks later, Lawrence wanted Ebony so desperately to move in with him that he provided her with a key to his apartment. Ebony thought it was just too soon. She did, however, enjoy the sex they shared. She thought, "I'm making up for lost time." Their sexual escapades had them humping like bunny rabbits nearly eight times a day! The two would meet up at Lawrence's for lunch, (not to eat) but for a rendezvous. She tried to take it slow, but it seemed like things were moving so fast that she couldn't keep up. Ebony did enjoy the pleasure that he was giving her body. It was official, Ebony was sprung! Lawrence was doing things to her body that felt oh so good!

Lawrence and Ebony had been hot and heavy since they first met, that she thought it was really love this time around. It didn't seem like he was the average Joe Blow. He was kind, attentive and caring, she thought. Lawrence was not like the others, he wanted to spend every waking moment with her. They seem to be inseparable. Not a moment of fresh air could come between them, because they were always together. He seemed like he had the qualities of that knight-in-shining armor that comes into your world, swoops down and rescues you. Lawrence started cooking dinner everyday and doing whatever it was that she asked of him. This made girl feel like she was on cloud nine. It seemed as if he was trying to be around for the long haul, (not just the usual booty call that she was used to.)

Ebony was on the ride of her life. Never in a million years did she ever think that she would find a man so attentive to her needs. Always wanting to be around her, doing things for her. She definitely wasn't use to this kind of treatment. She began to like this more than she could ever imagine.

Pressure is a mutha fucka! Ebony finally gave into Lawrence's pleas for her to move some of her things into his place. Shortly after being there, one morning, Ebony was awakened by the phone. She answered half asleep: a woman's voice replied on the other end. The woman introduced herself as Sheila, Lawrence's wife! Sheila asked Ebony "Do you live there?" In a sleeping daze, Ebony looked over at the closet and saw some of her things and told Sheila "yes". Both of them were silent, till Ebony broke the ice. She told Sheila that she would inform Lawrence that she had called. This call jolted Ebony from her sleep after she hung up. Ebony didn't know what to think! At no time did she ever think that her man, Mr. Knight-in-Shining Armor, was married!

Later that evening, she confronted him about the situation. He stated, "I told you that in the beginning". Now Ebony could recall all the stuff that Lawrence ever did for her and to her, but at no time did she recall him saying "I am married." Lawrence explained that he was only married to Sheila on paper and had not been with her in over two years.

Considering all the time and effort she had invested already into this relationship, Ebony asked Lawrence was there a divorce in sight. Lawrence assured her that he would do everything in his power to make that happened. He wanted to spend the rest of his life with her and to have children.

That night while preparing for bed, Lawrence made passionate love to Ebony to reassure her that he was only in love with her. While being intimate, Lawrence whispered into Ebony's ear, "Baby, I love you and want you to have my seed." The tears streamed down Ebony's face, as she felt the passion and desire. She had really fallen head over heels for this wonderful man. Not even a wife would stand in the way of her and her man! At that moment, Ebony decided that it was time to let the birth control pills go in the trashcan. They were the happy and inseparable couple.

She was waiting for Lawrence to return home from work, when a call came to the house. This time it was some "chicken head" telling Ebony that Lawrence was into her. Ebony explained to the young lady, that if he was so much into her, then she would have a key and not Ebony. A one way heated argument ensued and Ebony introduced her to "Mr. Click." Ebony was not about to waste her time and energy arguing with someone she didn't know. It was already bad enough that he had a wife, now someone else wanted to enter the picture. She didn't think that the girl got the picture, because she called right back. Ebony really didn't have time for this type of foolishness. She knew in her heart that she was there for a sole purpose. This time before Ebony hung up the phone; she told the girl, "come by the apartment if you so big, bad and want to sell wolf tickets!" One thing she learned from her mother and step father, never let anyone walk over you.

Later that night when she confronted Lawrence about the girl, he played it off. He told her that nothing was going on with that young lady. He never went into details about the girl and said, "Dismiss the whole issue and let's move on. You are here with me aren't you?"

Two days after the conversation with the unknown female, Ebony was on her way to medical. It had been two months since she had stopped taking the birth control pills. It appeared that Lawrence had gotten his wish, Ebony thought she was pregnant! After the previous year's tragedy of her loss, the glow in her face brought great joy. Just thinking that she might be carrying a bundle of joy took the hurt and pain away! "This man really cares and he wants to be there for me and the baby." she thought.

Once arriving to medical to take a pregnancy test, Ebony saw Lawrence outside with a young lady. Before stepping out the truck, she needed to get her head together. "This could be a co-worker, don't over react girl." Walking towards the front door, Ebony looked at him and he looked at her, but he never acknowledged her. At that moment, she was mad as hell. The steam was coming from her nostrils as she went inside to get tested. It was like the life had been ripped right from underneath her. Her man couldn't even acknowledge her! "Everyday, all day except for work, this man is in my grill." Today of all days, she couldn't even break his concentration!

After taking the test, the results came back negative. And after what had just happened, boy was she happy. When she left medical, Ebony noticed Lawrence was still outside chatting with this woman. Once again, Ebony made eye contact to see if he would acknowledge her. Nothing! Ebony sort of played it off and went straight for her vehicle. Hell naw! Ebony wasn't a sucker and she wasn't gonna let shit go down like that! She put the truck in neutral and hopped out. Ebony walked up to Lawrence and hurled his keys at him, then drove off. The thought ran thru her mind again that it was a blessing she wasn't pregnant! This man that she was falling for wouldn't even acknowledge her.

Later that night, Lawrence called with some bullshit excuse that this young lady didn't mean anything to him. Ebony stated, "I couldn't tell, since you didn't even introduce us." She felt as though any person that came around had a right to know her man, and vice versa. Deep in her heart it was like he was hiding something from her. Ebony just couldn't put her finger on it. If she was going to continue with this relationship, communication would have to play a major part.

He was so adamant about her coming back to his place that he drove to her place through the snow. They chatted the night away and he convinced her that that kind of action would never happen again. "Was that the girl that was arguing with Ebony?" "Was he trying to protect her?" She was a grown ass woman and she could handle her own!

To smooth things over, Lawrence made love to her, like his life depended on it. Ebony wasn't use to a man pressing on her and begging her to come back to them. The next day she returned back to Lawrence's place. If only Ebony could open up her eyes and see the blinders that were before her.

Things in the couple's lives were suppose to get better, not worse! One evening, the phone rang while Lawrence was watching television. Before Ebony had a chance to answer it, Lawrence had grabbed the receiver. He had the phone up to his ear as he made his way into their bedroom. Ebony was just laying there as her man looked into her eyes. Tears began to stream down his face; she didn't want to be rude, so she waited. She didn't know who was on the other end and what was making him cry. Thoughts ran through her mind that something happened to his mother or one of his sisters. After the call ended, she asked him what was going on, but he never answered. Ebony took it upon herself to hit the previous number listed on the phone log. She was on the line with Sheila, his wife. Ebony was most pleasant about the situation, but wanted to know from Sheila what was said that made him cry. Sheila stated, "That is for him to tell you. " No harsh words were passed between them, but Ebony explained that she had been taking care of Lawrence for a while and please do not disrupt their household. Granted that they were still married, but in all actuality, he was living with Ebony. Lawrence finally got himself together and told Ebony that Sheila was pregnant by someone else.

For the life of Ebony, it didn't make sense! "How could a man cry for someone that he hadn't been with in over two years?" she thought. Things didn't add up in her mind. This prompted her to get to the root of the problem. She resorted to snooping. It was like he had a lot of things to hide from her. He wasn't being truthful about his situation.

Every time she was left in the apartment alone, she went through his personal things. Ebony knew that this was invading his privacy, but it seemed like the only way to get to the bottom of it. Unpaid bills one after another were stuffed in his coat pockets. She uncovered a phone bill with a list of collect calls. Since she had been staying there and answering the phone, none had ever come thru. This made her dumbstruck. "Lawrence seemed to always have money in his pockets!" He didn't have a problem spending it on Ebony at all. "Why wasn't he paying his bills on time?"

After the crying episode, this put a spark under Lawrence and he had Ebony jumping through every hoop to give him a child. Ebony started going to the doctor's every week to be given one remedy after another. First it was prescribed for her to drink Robitussin to ensure that it would help improve cervical mucus for conception. Then it was the hormone drug,

Clomid, which was often used to induce ovulation. What she thought was the last and final remedy was to have surgery, a D&C, and she would be pregnant within six months. The surgery never took place because her doctor wanted to do the procedure at his local hospital. The cost would have doubled and the military was not willing to pay the added expense.

Thinking back on it, Ebony was pregnant the year before. She didn't have to go thru all this trouble. The problem with conception must have been her man. Considering how invested she was with this man, she did these things because she really cared for him. She desperately wanted a bundle of joy and he did also.

Chapter 3

That summer, Lawrence and Ebony ventured to Las Vegas, something that he had never done. Ebony wanted to show him all that she had learned during her course of travels. The traveling was like second nature to Ebony. Ever since a child, she traveled. The military had just intensified that passion even more. Lawrence had been in the military five years longer than she had, but never traveled out of the country. His only explorations were Illinois, Portsmouth and Warminster where the two had met.

Being a good manager of money, she set them on a budget for every night that they were to stay. The first day there, the couple explored the hotel. They wanted to see all that it had to offer. The Palace Station was tucked off of the strip. Granted it was not a big name brand hotel on the strip, it was very classy. The hotel had provided them with coupons for breakfast, dinner and cocktails. This would help them in the long run to cut down on the cost of food.

Lawrence was so in a hurry to gamble. Ebony was in no rush, she had been gambling since the age of four. Her father's family had her playing cards at an early age. The couple went there separate ways and had planned to meet at five o'clock for dinner. Before Ebony could even sit down and play a few hands of blackjack, Lawrence was standing over her wanting more money.

"No one is to ever take money off of your stack of chips while playing", Ebony thought. She was not use to this while gambling. Her father's side of the family gambled and when someone stands over you, it brings bad luck. Ebony finally removed herself from the game, because she could no longer keep her rhythm. He had broken that.

The two walked over to the slots, where Ebony gave Lawrence some more of her money. As the two sat side by side, she inserted five quarters and hit the jackpot. His eyes lit up like a Christmas tree. He wanted to spend more, but Ebony wasn't willing to give it back to the casino. Always listening to what was instilled in her as a child; Ebony decided to take the winnings and buy Lawrence his wedding ring. She really wanted him to marry her there, but that is what you called being blinded by love. He was not even divorced yet.

The couple enjoyed five glorious days in the sun. They even ventured off and drove to Arizona. They made it to Hoover Dam, where it was hot as hell. Ebony had never experienced that kind of heat before. Yes Guam, Thailand and even Vegas were hot, but Arizona took it to another level. There really wasn't a lot to see, but they did learn about how the dam was built. Ebony and Lawrence were ever so grateful to leave and drive back to Vegas. She really did enjoy this vacation. The only problem that she had was how he burned thru the money and fucked up the budget.

Ebony tried her best to let him be the man, but it was hard. It was like his upbringing didn't teach him how to be a real man. They both had their own unique styles and taste. The feeling of opposite's attract must have gravitated during this course of romance, because all these signs she clearly ignored.

Early fall, the couple decided to travel to the mall one particular evening. They were in search of a wedding ring for the bride to be. While at Kay Jeweler's, Ebony saw the most beautiful full carat ring she had ever seen. She really wasn't into diamonds, but could not resist this ring. The band was woven and she really had to have it. During the course of purchasing it, Lawrence was denied credit. Ebony had to charge her own wedding set! She should have known right then and there something was up. "The fucked up stuff women do, just to be with a man", she thought.

They arrived at TGI Friday's for dinner. After ordering food and drinks, Lawrence got down on one knee and proposed to her. Ebony had dreamt about this moment most of her adult life. Yes, Yes, I will marry you. She was so elated that she could hardly wait to call home to tell her parents that she was engaged to be married.

Ebony finally brought Lawrence home to meet her mother, stepfather and grandmother. They welcomed him with open arms. Barbara, Ebony's grandmother, thought of Lawrence as her extended grandson. Ebony was shocked, because a year earlier she had brought home a friend, and Barbara spoke and went straight upstairs. She later stated, "It was something about him that she didn't like."

For some reason, Barbara was elated with the presence of Lawrence. All the years Ebony grew up in her mother and grandmother's house, she never had anyone spend the night. Barbara was from the old school and you were not allowed to sleep together if you weren't married. But for some reason while on their visit, Barbara condoned the situation. Ebony figured it was because she now had an engagement ring on her finger. Lawrence had this halo around him, like he was the perfect gentlemen. The whole family began to really think that Ebony had found herself a winner.

Ebony had her heart set on becoming Mrs. Lawrence Richmond. Ebony gave Lawrence five hundred dollars for the divorce to Sheila. She did not let her grandmother know that Lawrence was married, she kept it a secret. Once again not wanting to disappoint her family, Ebony did what she thought was best.

Lawrence did file for divorce, but for some apparent reason the papers became missing in action. Ebony even contacted Sheila, Lawrence's soon to be ex to ask if she received them. Sheila explained that she had received the papers, but she did not have money to send them back. Ebony took it one step further and told Lawrence that he needed to send Sheila a money order, so that she could return the divorce papers. Ebony pressured him constantly. She just didn't want to have her wedding date come and the divorce wasn't final.

The countless delays with the divorce paperwork probably were a sign from God. But really, no one can see what they are supposed to see when they are wearing blinders. She had numerous warnings in front of her. For starters there was the smothering, the big lie, not acknowledging her, crying over his ex, rushing to get Ebony pregnant, the mismanagement of money and poor ass credit.

Before meeting Lawrence, Ebony had her own brand new vehicle. She wasn't really looking to upgrade, since she had what she wanted. Lawrence refused to drive it because it was a stick. So every time they went to Baltimore, they would drive his "little hoopty." Even when the couple went on vacation with Leroy, Vanessa, and Barbara to Virginia Beach, Lawrence drove his car. Out of the blue, he persuaded her to trade in her truck for a car. Ebony couldn't afford the higher payments. He decided that he would help her pay the other half of what she was lacking for the new payment. Technically, she was fine with what she had, but wanted to make her man happy.

This particular night, they arrived at the Toyota dealership. Ebony knew that it would not be a problem getting a new car, because she had

A1 credit. The salesperson ran her credit; since the banks were closed, he told Ebony that she could take the car home. Everything was ok and all she had to do was come back the next afternoon and sign papers. At that instance, Ebony thought she saw signs that Lawrence was jealous. The look in his eyes pierced through her soul as if to cut her down. He was jealous because: (1.) His name could not be on the loan, (2.) How the salesperson let her take the car. Little did she know that something detrimental had begun.

Thanksgiving was fast approaching and Lawrence wanted Ebony to meet his mother. Ebony did not want to go there without a peace offering. It seemed like every time she chatted with Lawrence's mother over the phone, Ebony picked up a vibe. People have said that mothers are very protective of their only son. So, Ebony really just brushed it off. To make amends for the situation, Ebony set off to the jewelry store and purchased a gold bracelet to smooth things over.

After driving the new ride to Missouri over twenty-two hours, the two of them made it safely. It seemed as if the people there were pleasant and very friendly. Everyone seemed to wave at you when driving by. After approaching his mother's home, everyone greeted each other with a warm gesture.

Elizabeth gave up her room for her only son. Ebony couldn't believe it. The real astonishment was that Elizabeth gave them clean towels everyday. Lawrence didn't care where he was, he wanted sex. Ebony felt uncomfortable; the house was small and he wanted to fuck as if they were home! Not wanting to cause no drama, Ebony gave in. She guessed Elizabeth could hear them in the bedroom every night that was why she was so thoughtful with the linen.

During the trip, Ebony began to see that Lawrence did whatever his mother asked of him. Ebony felt out of place, "Lawrence, what a nice car you have", "I need to go here, and I need to go there." It seemed like when he got around his family, he was like the big baller. She had had enough and told Lawrence that they could not afford to purchase dinner every night for four adults and four children. She asked that he take her to the supermarket so she could cook verses buying dinner. It wasn't as if Lawrence and Ebony were the only adults in the home, even though one of his sisters also lived there with her two children. Granted he was the only boy; Ebony thought, they relied too much on him.

After the majority of the family arrived, the house became a zoo. People were all over the place sleeping on the floor and the couches. It seemed like every nook and cranny had a person lying around. Ebony was awe struck because she never lived like that. She figured they were use to this arrangement. At that particular time, she was grateful that she had a room to sleep in.

A while later after Thanksgiving dinner, it was time to make the long trip back home. Before they could leave, one of his sisters asked for some cash to get home, and of course, he gave it to her. All their money was depleted and they barely had enough for gas to return back to Pennsylvania. Lawrence really didn't care, because he knew that his fiancé would use her credit cards. Little did Ebony know that the window was wide open for her to look and see what was going on, but she dismissed the signs again. Just the thought of having a man excited her.

Since the couple spent Thanksgiving with his family, Ebony thought it would only be fair to spend Christmas with her family. Lawrence didn't seem to have a problem with this, but there was a little hesitation at first. He was shocked and surprised to see how well Ebony's family really catered to him and welcomed him as part of the family. This sort of eased the tension, so the couple drove to Baltimore on Christmas Eve.

While Lawrence slept, Ebony crept upstairs and went into her mother's room. She retrieved all the gifts she had for Lawrence and made it to the living room. As the morning came and Lawrence had awaken, Christmas morning he found that all his gifts from Ebony were laid all over the love seat.

Ebony's mother use to do this for her as a child. Not saying that he was her child, but she wanted him to enjoy the experience she had. Clearly during the visit to his mother's home, Ebony could see that the whole family wasn't use to anything. Lawrence couldn't believe that his woman really cared for him. She had purchased her man: clothes, a watch, underwear, cologne and a jacket. Before leaving for dinner, he received gifts from Ebony's mother and grandmother. The expression on his face said a thousand words. He became speechless and glassy eyed. Ebony wasn't really concerned about how much he gave her. She just enjoyed the expression on his face.

The couple went downstairs and prepared themselves for dinner over her aunt's house. This is where he would really meet the rest of the family. Vanessa's side of the family was a little close knit group of twelve. They weren't loud or obnoxious like her father's side of the family or Lawrence's for that matter.

After arriving over her aunt's house for dinner, it was not chaos like

Thanksgiving dinner. Lawrence was introduced to the clan and he was welcomed. The family joined hands and held prayer before eating. Each person said what they were thankful for during that particular holiday season. The spread was fabulous; Ebony's family really knew how to burn.

Dinner had concluded and it was now finally time for the exchanging of gifts. Lawrence thought that he would be excluded, because the family was just meeting him. Little did he know that he was not left out. They showered him with gifts. He went outside and cried. He stated, "I never would have imagined how well they made me feel." Lawrence told Ebony that Sheila's family never liked him at all and would have never done anything like that. By the looks of his mother's home and where he was from, she could clearly see that he was not use to anything. Ebony was upgrading this man minute by minute, something that she would regret later down the line.

Chapter 4

Finally on February 07, 1994, Lawrence was officially divorced from Shelia. On February 14, 1994, in the Commonwealth State of Pennsylvania, Ebony became Mrs. Lawrence Richmond. She really didn't want to have her wedding on Valentine's Day but on her cousin's birthday two days later. That date was not available. Ebony was so anxious, that it didn't matter as long as she became Mrs. Richmond. Vanessa had called her that morning to congratulate the couple. Vanessa loved her daughter so much; she brought her whole wedding attire for Valentine's Day.

Ebony's shipmate that lived next door and her boyfriend were witnesses at the J.O.P. The couple also threw the newly married couple a reception in the barracks. There was plenty of food and drinks. Lawrence drank himself into a drunken stupor. Regardless of how drunk he was, he never lost on the pool table. This man had skills ruling the table. Sadly it was clear, no one who worked with him showed up. Ebony was so grateful to the couple that stood up for them and her other shipmates that worked with her.

She had also been planning a large wedding in her hometown. Ebony had already been preparing for her upcoming nuptials, set for the summer '94. She had been to visit her hometown to discuss the details with her mom and stepfather. Vanessa put in overtime constantly to make sure her one and only child had the most gorgeous wedding she could afford. Ebony loved her mother dearly and knew that having the wedding on her birthday would make things worthwhile. This would be a special day for her; her anniversary and her mother's birthday.

As the time moved closer, Ebony chose her bridesmaids and wanted to know if Lawrence had anyone that he wanted in the wedding. Lawrence had no friends that would vouch for him on his big day. Ebony didn't think anything of it, so she enlisted the help of her family. Her male cousins from both sides of the family stepped up to help out. It was fun for Ebony to make visits and go shopping with her mother and family. They chose gowns and Ebony paid for all the girls' shoes and brought the guys a little something for helping out.

Ebony could see that her mother was working extra hard to make this a special event. She didn't want her to spend so much; she decided that she would help out in anyway possible. While in Pennsylvania, Ebony picked out her own wedding gown and purchased it. The only person that was allowed to see her in it was Vanessa when she came to visit. Vanessa thought that her daughter had picked out a fabulous gown, but only had one complaint. She wanted the gown much longer; the store had no problem altering the dress to Vanessa's satisfaction.

Also, Ebony wanted this to be a fairy tale. She had read in a Jet magazine, how Whitney Houston and Bobby Brown had live doves at their wedding. Ebony thought that if they could, why couldn't she? She got busy in the yellow pages to find a place in Baltimore that provided that kind of service. It didn't take her long, and a person provided her all the information. It only cost $500 to make her fantasy a reality. That was a small price to pay for something so unique.

The bride had over two hundred and fifty guest attend the ceremony. The attending people from Lawrence's family were his mother and one sister. Without thinking back on how his mother Elizabeth had reacted to her, Ebony felt as though she had died and gone to heaven. At the end of the night, Lawrence's sister and mother gave her a wedding gift bag and said, "Oh, I forgot and left the gift in Missouri". This was a shock, but what made Ebony really upset on her big day, was having her new mother-in-law and sister-in-law ride in the car with her on the way to the hotel. They refused a ride from anyone else, stating that only Lawrence could take them back to Vanessa's house. Ebony couldn't believe all that had transpired. And what topped it off was that she had sent Elizabeth money to buy a dress and a plane ticket to attend the wedding. Elizabeth showed up wearing a dress she had wore to one of her daughter's wedding. Heavenly bliss or was it! Ebony was sure that Elizabeth didn't do this with any of her other six daughters.

After the vows, and getting to the hotel, Ebony was steaming! Lawrence made excuses that they didn't know anyone, which was why he did what he did. She couldn't rationalize him driving to two gas stations to buy a soda for Elizabeth. That was over the top! But what would happen next?

Lawrence said to Ebony, "Bitch, I got you now!" Ebony blocked it out, because she couldn't believe what she had just heard and what had just taken place in the car. While at the wedding the couple had received money from the money dance. Her family and friends had shown much support. She divided the money in half even though no support came from his family.

The next day the couple arrived at Vanessa's house where they had left their toothbrushes. Before they got out the car, Ebony stated to Lawrence that they were not doing anything for anyone. They were there to brush their teeth and go out to brunch. While exiting the car, Vanessa yelled up the street "Hello, married couple". When Vanessa walked into the house, Lawrence was upstairs talking to Elizabeth. The next thing, Lawrence was leaving out the door to get McDonalds for his family. Vanessa and Ebony could not believe it.

Later that night, while the couple was opening their wedding gifts, Elizabeth and her daughter batted their eyes in jealousy. It was the same look Lawrence gave her when he couldn't get credit. Go figure, they were family!

Before returning back to Missouri, Ebony and Lawrence decided to take his family on a tour of Baltimore. They took the family to the Inner Harbor and the Aquarium. Lawrence foot the bill the whole time. At no time did Elizabeth or her daughter pay for a thing. At the completion of their trip, Lawrence had run out of his portion of money and wanted some of Ebony's.

The happy couple returned back to Warminster to prepare for their honeymoon. Vanessa and Leroy were to meet the couple in Atlantic City after a few days in the Pocono Mountains. The room had a heart shaped bed, jacuzzi tub, personal swimming pool and a sauna in the room. The grounds were very pretty. Ebony was tired of all the sexing and just needed some much needed rest. Most mornings, she couldn't even get out of the bed. She did however make it to dinner most nights. The two went range shooting and long walks. They spent most of their time in the room using all of her bridal gifts from her party.

Three worthwhile days. AC here we come! The couple was supposed to meet Ebony's parents in Caesar's Palace. After spending over the amount allotted, they decided to leave. Ebony couldn't find her mother and step father and was sort of disappointed. Arriving home getting settled in, a knock came at the door. Her parents had finally caught up with them. Ebony was exhausted, but glad to be in the company of real family.

Things began to move quickly for her, Ebony started to upgrade Lawrence's apartment. She didn't want anything to remind them of Sheila, and the first to go was the mattress and box spring. She had practically revamped his whole apartment, trying to get rid of any trace of him being married before. She had expensive taste on an economical budget with a touch of class. The most expensive thing that they got was of Lawrence's picking, an entertainment center for $3000. Ebony tried to reason with logic, that they were married. It was now we instead of me.

One thing came right after another it seemed. Detecting jealousy since Ebony had a new ride, he now needed a car. Once again, they set off for the dealer. Ebony thought that she had to get him one, because their checks were now in the same bank account. At first she was trying to maintain both accounts, but it got a little time consuming.

While at the dealer, Lawrence decided on a used Toyota Camry. Once again he became upset because Ebony had to put it in her name. Considering he was the man, Ebony thought that he would inspect the car before purchasing it. It seemed that after they pulled off the lot, the car all of a sudden need four new tires. Ebony called on her cousin that was in her wedding, he owned a garage. The money that he gave them for a wedding present was now being returned with more added for the new tires. For all of Ebony's family and friends support, and none from Lawrence's, he used all the wedding money for his gain and not as a unit.

Chapter 5

The first year of marriage was starting off rocky. Lawrence and Ebony worked in such close proximity to one another that he would not let her drive to work. They began to ride to work, eat lunch, and then take the daily trip back home together. I guess the signs were dancing around in Ebony's head; "Can I breathe on my own?" All the clothing that she wore before they got married, he told her, she could no longer wear. "Being a wife now, you need to give them miniskirts up."

Ebony did the unthinkable and decided that maybe they should attend counseling. This should have been done prior to getting married. Lawrence put up a major fight, but finally gave in. While attending counseling, Lawrence felt as though the counselor and Ebony were ganging up on him. They each had a chance to express views of how the other felt.

Ebony's only complaint was that she couldn't breath and sometimes needed time to herself. Also, she felt that Lawrence spent money like it grew on trees! Lawrence's complaint was that Ebony would not let him be a man and spend his money the way that he wanted to. With the counselor's help, Ebony gave into a set budget that Lawrence could take out every payday. Lawrence seemed to lighten up a little and the relationship was going fine, or so she thought.

The only requirement she had for her husband was that he let her know when he spent something with a check. She wasn't trying to manage how he spent it, but tried to make sure the checkbook balanced. Later, Ebony had received a letter from the bank stating that a check had bounced. This would be the first bounced check she would incur in her life! Lawrence's excuse was, "Oh! I forgot."

Ebony never really had a lot of girlfriends. So at her new job, she was approached by some girls that told her, she was acting antisocial. Ebony explained that she wasn't one to approach people, but had no problem speaking or hanging out every now and then. As time went on, they began to do aerobics together and wanted to just hang out.

One night while Lawrence was at work, Ebony called to let him know that she would be stepping out with her co-worker. Lawrence "pitched a bitch" and stated "Why you going somewhere when I am at work? " Ebony explained to him, last time she checked they were both equal in this marriage. She had a right to have friends just as he did. Since her paycheck contributed to the rent, she was entitled to come and go also. Little did she know, but at that moment she became a prisoner in her own home. She buckled down and did not go out that night.

Ebony was one to try and keep the peace. Even as a child, she did not like to keep trouble brewing in the air. Her co-worker finally stopped hanging around because of Lawrence's possessiveness. Every person that Ebony tried to befriend ran into the same thing. One day she thought that she would invite a co-worker, his girlfriend and their son for dinner. Big mistake! It turned out after they left; Lawrence accused Ebony of having an affair with her coworker. He did not want her being around males or females. Ebony was his prize possession trophy and no one was allowed to look or touch but him.

While at work, Ebony ran into a childhood friend. Trina used to be in a marching band with her. Being very excited about seeing someone from home, she decided to invite Trina over whenever she came to town. Lawrence seemed like he had no problem with Trina coming once a month. One weekend while Trina was visiting, she suggested that they attend Fairmount Park for the Greek Picnic. It was an annual event for celebrating African American college fraternities and sororities. Ebony was so excited that Lawrence had given her permission to go. It seemed like when people were around them, he acted like Ebony could do anything that she wanted. When Trina left, Lawrence would scold her as if she was a child. Trina could sense that things were not right and she did not want to interfere, so she never went back to their home again.

While visiting Ebony's family in Baltimore, family members wanted to know when a bundle of joy would be on the way. Ebony made excuse after excuse that she had the problem, when in all actuality it was Lawrence. His sperm count was really low and hard for him to produce children. It seemed like Ebony protected her man at every cost. The final thing for Ebony to do was invitro fertilization. Ebony was so scared of needles that she came up with another option to adopt. Lawrence was hell bent on getting a baby girl, but Ebony stated that they needed to get what God would want them to have, a healthy baby. She got busy with her homework to find children through the National Adoption Center. You would not believe all the children that were waiting for a loving home. Ebony thought that this would really help Lawrence to calm down if he had a family of his own. After months of looking for the right child and training classes for preparation of adoption, their wish would soon come true.

Since they had to wait a minute, a trip would never hurt or would it? After receiving the mail one day, an advertisement to travel four locations intrigued Lawrence. She knew that it had to be a quick scheme gimmick. Lawrence was excited because that meant going somewhere else, since he never traveled like his wife. When Lawrence made the call, Ebony knew there would be a catch. To enjoy this vacation you had to pay for your own airfare and hotel taxes. Lawrence pumped her up and forced her to make a decision on the spot. Since he was so excited, Ebony once again used her credit card to hold their reservations. Lawrence was supposed to have the spending money.

The couple drove to Vanessa's home, where in turn she drove them to Dulles Airport. The adventure of a lifetime was on the horizon, Orlando, West Palm Beach, Bahamas, Daytona and finally New Orleans. The trip was a success as long as Lawrence was able to spend money. He did not stay on budget and by the time they arrived in New Orleans, they had blown the budget! Ebony just wanted to go home, and bad! She missed the comfort of her own bed. She had started using credit cards to support the rest of the vacation. Ebony had had all that she could take. This would be the last and final trip the couple would ever take in her mind.

Chapter 6

The couple received a phone call in early summer of 1995. It was the adoption agency stating that they had the perfect match for them. It was a little healthy baby boy! His parents could not afford to take care of him, because they had four other children. The agency provided the Richmond's with a photo of their soon to be son. Ebony knew deep down in her heart that this was the right child. It was just something about his fat little cheeks and his smooth baby skin. Most importantly his birthday was the day after her mother's.

Ebony was so excited, that when it came time for the family 4th of July cookout at Gunpowder State Park, she took her picture of her little man with her. She was already a proud momma and hadn't even seen her new son yet. Vanessa was once again proud that she was going to become a grandmother. Everyone in Ebony's family was ecstatic; she had been married now, but no pregnancies.

Before the baby could arrive, Lawrence received a call and learned that Elizabeth was getting married. Ebony scrambled to impress her mother in law. She wanted things to work out this time around. Ebony brought ribbon in Elizabeth's colors and made bows for the wedding. Before making it there, their trip became rocky.

Lawrence wanted a truck now, because they were getting their baby boy soon. Ebony stated that if he wanted a truck he would have to get it on his own. He had just got a car last year. Ebony didn't know you could just change cars like you changed your drawers. He set out to do it on his own, but called Ebony and stated that she needed to sign some papers. When Ebony refused, all hell broke loose. Lawrence came home ranting and raving that she didn't love him. All he wanted her to do was sign some damn papers for him to get what he wanted. Ebony knew that she was way in over her head in debt, and to keep bailing Lawrence out could not continue. She had already used a credit card to pay for two years worth of back taxes that Lawrence didn't file!

As the Richmond's set off on this long journey again, they really were not speaking to one another. While there, Ebony met all of her sister-in-laws. It seemed that they were there just to party. Lawrence and Ebony did pull it together to save face for the family. Ebony ended up coordinating Elizabeth's whole wedding and making her veil. It was like she took control of the situation and Lawrence took control of the cooking. The sisters were no assistance at all. Lawrence still was not a happy camper. The couple did pull it together for his mother's wedding. It turned out to be a success.

Elizabeth was grateful for Ebony's help. Ebony couldn't believe that her mother-in-law was finally coming around to her. She was still however upset about what Elizabeth did to her on her wedding day, but decided to let it go. The new married couple thanked the Richmond's with lunch. This gave Lawrence a chance to chat with his new stepfather.

After returning from Missouri, Lawrence was at it again about that damn truck. Ebony tried to explain that she was over extended in debt now and it was mission impossible. The following day, Lawrence took it upon himself to go out and find some shady deal and Ebony was stuck with signing the papers after all. Lawrence got his wish and got a used Trooper that year. He had just gotten the Camry last year and invested money for tires. "What would happen with this Trooper now?" Ebony thought.

On August 11, 1995, was the most joyous day of Ebony's life. Lawrence and Ebony Richmond set out on a journey to Silver Spring, Maryland to pick up their new son. It seemed that everything that could go wrong went wrong. Before arriving there, the Richmond's forgot the baby bag with clothes. Lawrence wanted to forge on ahead because they were in Delaware during rush hour traffic. Ebony knew that they had to return, because they had to spend major bank to get this baby. The couple finally made it safely and on time after doubling back. Ebony couldn't believe how special he was! The couple decided to change the baby's name to Shawn and the rest followed after his new father.

On the way back, they decided to stop through Baltimore. Vanessa was excited and called her mother Barbara; before you knew it everyone was there to see the new addition to the family. When the couple returned back to Philly, things began to change again. Ebony took off time from work to bond with Shawn, but it seemed like since he had been in the home he only wanted Lawrence's attention. Shawn slept on Lawrence's side of the bed. Anytime he cried, Lawrence was there to baby him. On numerous well baby visits, the doctor advised Ebony that if she didn't nip this in the bud soon, no one would want to baby-sit. Ebony tried her hardest to explain this to Lawrence, but his new focus was his son. At that moment he excluded anything and anyone who got in his way. He did not let Ebony do anything for the baby, except make bottles and get him dressed for the babysitters in the morning. She could not even really say anything to their son. At that moment, she felt as though the roles had reversed. Lawrence was now the mother and she was the father.

Vanessa was so ecstatic that her baby girl and son-in-law had made her a grandma. She threw a baby shower and the family gathered to support the couple. Shawn was not lacking for anything. One thing about Vanessa, she was not a talker but a person that acted. Unlike Elizabeth, who only sent Shawn a few items.

Since Shawn had come into Ebony's life, she felt that she needed to become more domesticated. Ebony took up baking; she was determined to bake his first birthday cake. She became an active parent in his daycare and always baked treats just because. This became her hustle, when money got short she would sell cookies at daycare and her job. Ebony also took up hemming and pressing clothes for people at work. It was fine to Lawrence because he just wanted to sit back and play with Shawn.

In Ebony's mind, Lawrence didn't seem like he was all bad. He made sure that every birthday or holiday she would get whatever it was she was into that year. Be it tools to decorate cakes, a new foot massager, wax machine, or her favorite the Kitchen Aid mixer. Ebony was known for always trying to save a dollar by getting it done herself.

Christmas was a joyous occasion! The family gathered in Baltimore for Shawn's first Christmas. He was so adorable, dressed in his little red "baby's first Christmas" outfit. Ebony set her baby under the tree like he was a present, and Lawrence took plenty of pictures. It seemed like the couple was happy but deep inside Ebony was screaming for help. She wanted so bad to tell her mother what was going on with the sexing constantly and not being able to do anything on her own. Ebony couldn't bring herself to do it. Ebony had begun to hide the pain and anguish she felt for Lawrence.

The only time Ebony got quality time to herself was the supermarket. She made sure that she went through each and every isle; just to be away from home for over two hours. After arriving home with the groceries and hauling them in the house, she still had to maintain her wifely duties. Sex had become like a chore to her. Since they were married and Shawn was there, Lawrence didn't need to do it eight times a day. Ebony felt that he had her now, and once would suffice. Of course he didn't see it that way.

Shawn's first birthday was approaching and it took his mother a whole week to prepare the ensemble. She had prepared a clown cake, with cookies for his name. There were clown cookies topping rice crispy treats for each child to take home. Vanessa hired a family friend to play a clown for the children. After arriving in Baltimore for Shawn's party, her cousin thought that she had purchased the cake from Sam's. The party was a big success! The clown blew balloons and the children had a great time. As the party came to a close, the family went to Vanessa's. Ebony's family always showed support and had Lawrence and Ebony's back.

Christmas was a few months away and Ebony was always preparing ahead of time. Every time Ebony and Lawrence needed anything or fell short for bill money, Ebony reached out to Vanessa. She wouldn't dare let Christmas come without giving her mother something special. They didn't have any money because Lawrence always spent it like it grew on trees. She had closed out most of her credit card accounts and cut up the all the actual cards, preparing to purchase a home. Her neighbor and Shawn's godmother told her that she could call the card company and explain that she had lost one of her cards and they would provide a new one. Ebony got on the phone to do just that.

Chapter 7

A week later, Ebony was just chilling at home. A quite evening with Lawrence and Shawn. They had just finished eating dinner, when Pamela called for Ebony to pick up a piece of mail. She had intercepted the mail so that Lawrence would not see it. When Ebony left to go next door and return, Lawrence wanted to know what it was all about. Ebony replied, nothing important just a piece of mail that I was looking for. Little did she know that the Pamela had already given Lawrence an insight of what it was, a credit card. Ebony never knew that this result would come about over a credit card that was in her name and not his. She was known for digging his ass out of a ditch.

Before Ebony could blink good, Lawrence wrapped his strong hand around Ebony's slim neck and lifted her up off the floor with one hand. Her feet were dangling in mid air. Her eyes bulged and salvia streamed from her lips. "Don't you know I could kill you bitch! " Ebony was gasping for air, could feel consciousness slipping from her body. She had fear in her eyes because she had never seen her man react like this. The room became dark as midnight as Ebony held on to life. For the life of her, time was standing still. "How long before he really kills you?", she thought. "Bitch I will kill your ass!" Lawrence threatened. Just before she could pass out, Lawrence released his grip and stated "Don't ever do no shit like that again without my knowledge!"

Ebony tried to regain her composure and move out of his way before the violence started again. She didn't want to upset him in any other way. Ebony was scared as hell. It hurt for her just to swallow anything. She went into the bathroom and closed the door, scared to come out. She just looked at the bruises around her neck. Ebony couldn't and wouldn't be able to explain this to anyone. Lawrence was just a nice guy to everyone. Who would really believe her?

As time went on, Lawrence had calmed down like nothing had ever happened, and as they say it is all good in the hood. After picking up Shawn to get ready for bed, Lawrence demanded to have sex. With all that was going on Ebony was scared that if she did not have sex with her husband, another choking or a beating would be sure to follow. He was ruff and continued to thrust his manhood into her dry opening as if she was a piece of trash. Lawrence seemed like he was possessed by a demonic entity at that moment. She wanted to cry, but no sounds would escape her mouth. Ebony laid there helplessly while her husband violently raped her. She just let him finish handling his business. Afterwards, she just laid there and cried herself to sleep. The next day she really wanted to tell someone, but didn't have anyone to talk to because Lawrence controlled her every movement. She was not even allowed to chat with her family unless he was around. The following day, Lawrence awoke as if nothing ever happened. Ebony was speechless, because she felt like if she said the slightest thing, something else would jump off.

Chapter 8

After the initial assault, Ebony was scared; she wouldn't even tell her mother. Vanessa never got into the couple's business, but requested that Lawrence never hit her daughter.

Ebony decided that she needed to get away for the weekend, so she decided to go home. Since Lawrence never really like her being out of his sight, he would call about twenty times to check on her whereabouts. While there, a knock came at her mother's door around five o'clock in the morning. Who on earth could it be she thought? It was Shannon, a high school classmate of Ebony. Back in the day they hung out in school, but Shannon was into drugging at the time. Ebony wanted to know why she was out in the streets that time of the morning. Shannon explained that she needed ten dollars to send her daughter on a field trip. Not thinking anything of it, Ebony gave her the money. It wasn't as if Shannon had that far to go, they lived not too far from another.

During the next visit to Baltimore, Ebony decided to visit Shannon's grandmother to see how she was doing. Getting a real good glimpse of her, she knew that she was getting high and bad. Ebony trying to be the good samaritan that she was, offered to check out some facilities in Philly.

When she returned home, she told her husband what had happened on her latest visit. In the midst of her own problems the phone rang and to her surprise it was Shannon's baby's daddy on the line. He stated that Shannon needed to get away to get herself together. He wanted to know if she could come and stay, that he would provide whatever payment that was asked. Ebony spoke to Lawrence and surprisingly he said that Shannon could stay. It seemed like he had a soft heart all of a sudden. Shannon was on the bus that night. When she arrived, she had blotches all over her face and body.

Before Shannon's arrival, they moved Shawn back into their bedroom to give her some privacy. She enclosed herself in the room for two days; withdrawals had to have been something. Ebony sort of laid down some ground rules that Shannon had to get up and get a job. Even though her boyfriend was providing three hundred a month, she still needed to earn her keep for her own personal items. Ebony took Shannon to the mall to get her nails done and some makeup. Shannon refused any makeup stating that she wanted to be herself, take it or leave it. While at the mall, she had gotten some job applications. It seemed like every store she went into, they looked at Shannon like she was crazy. Not wanting to give her a complex, Ebony took it upon herself to start asking for the applications. They would take them home so that Shannon could fill them out.

Shannon had gotten better and started working at a local Rite Aid. Ebony had been to the store once or twice. Shannon had befriended this young man who was taking her to work. One morning Ebony had awakened to find the young man in her living room. She told Shannon that guests weren't allowed in the home at four thirty in the morning. It seemed that every time you turned around this guy was always around Shannon. Ebony didn't know it, but the guy was Shannon's new get high partner.

Lawrence was off work this particular day and Ebony had to work. When she returned home, she saw Lawrence walking around in his bathrobe. Only Lawrence and Shannon were home alone, Shawn had been at daycare. Ebony asked Lawrence to step inside the room because they needed to talk. She explained that he should never walk around undressed because they had Shannon living with them now. Ebony never thought much of the incident to later years. Love can be blind when you put all your energy and time trying to escape your own problems. Ebony was so focused on trying to help a so-called friend, that she didn't even see that her friend was sleeping with her man. People have said that what is done in the dark will come to light. Eventually it would be brought to Ebony's attention.

Chapter 9

The following fall of 97' it was time for Ebony and Lawrence to move. It was either the sunshine state of Florida or Virginia for lovers. Lawrence didn't want to go to Florida, because he would be away from Ebony and Shawn. They agreed that Virginia would be the best fit. Pamela watched over the house and kept Shawn while they headed to Virginia to search for a new home. While there they stayed with Lawrence's sister.

They found a perfect house, but since their finances were not in order they could not get it. See, what Ebony didn't know was that when you are married your credit report merges together. She was not used to getting turned down for anything. Vanessa had always instructed her that you can get credit, but whatever you use you must pay back. While in Virginia Beach, they ran into a local realtor who worked with them to find a place. He instructed them to go home and to come back on New Year's Day. Ebony really thought that the realtor was crazy because who would work on New Year's Day. True to form, he was legit and met them that day. They found a cute house to rent that would hold all of their furniture.

While preparing for the move, Shannon all of a sudden had to go out of the country, Spain. This meant that she wouldn't be of any help. Her baby daddy had called for her to come because he had broken his ankle. Vanessa as usual was in her daughter's corner and took the Greyhound up to be of assistance. The movers came and packed the house up and the couple left out a few things until they could get their stuff. The drive was a smooth one, but for some reason Ebony was getting nervous. After arriving, Vanessa went to work helping to get things squared away in the home. She took the couple to the store and advised that she would purchase them a washer and a dryer or a refrigerator. Ebony didn't want her mother to spend so much, she accepted the refrigerator. Even though they had to rent the house, they needed to supply those items. Leroy had a thing for Vanessa; he could sniff her out wherever she was. He knew that she had gone to help Ebony and that they were now in Virginia Beach, but didn't know where. By the second day there, Leroy was in Virginia Beach at the front door. Ebony was always amazed how her stepfather, Leroy could find them without even telling him how to get there. Maybe he had that calling on him, or he just loved his family so.

Two weeks had passed and who should call to say they needed a ride from the airport, but Shannon. She came back to an already fixed up house, not having to lift a finger. Ebony was very angry and thought how convenient. Lawrence had to go away for training, so she really couldn't stay mad at Shannon because she needed her assistance to help with Shawn. After her arrival, Ebony helped Shannon get her drivers license. This would help Ebony in a big way. This was short lived after Shannon was introduced to one of Lawrence's sisters. It seemed that she was spending the night there constantly, after her and Shannon hung out and partied. Ebony wondered what she really needed Shannon there for if she was going to have to do everything herself anyway. Ebony decided that she could do it on her own and put Shannon out. She didn't see why Shannon would rather sleep on someone's floor, than to have her own room.

The month was up and Lawrence was back in town. Since Shannon was now out of the house, the outburst became more and more frequent. Lawrence demanded sex all the time, when Ebony gave into his needs it was never good enough. Apparently, she had missed the fact that he was sexing Shannon and now taking out his frustrations on her. Ebony thought back to the beginning when they would make passionate love and then hold each other-those days were long gone. Lawrence always complained that she was not sexing him on the regular. Since Shawn had come into the picture, Ebony thought things were suppose to change a little. Not that being intimate with her husband was not important, but eight times a day was too much now. Lawrence was not trying to hear that, if she even missed one time out of the day, "It ain't like you giving it to me on the regular anyway."

Things were a little different now, because Ebony had a newfound independence. She worked in Norfolk and Lawrence worked in Newport News. She had her outlet because she could finally breathe. No more of waiting to go to the grocery store to breath, she could do it daily. Since the couple was not in each other's presence except for at home, all hell was about to break loose. No one knew that things could get any worse.

Since Ebony handled the bills, when she got their cell phone bill one particular number showed up on numerous occasions. When she approached Lawrence about it, he stated,"Oh, it is just a girl from work having problems with her man." Ebony told him that he needed to get his own house in order before counseling someone else. One day while bathing, this girl had the nerve to call the house. Ebony had to put a stop to it! Lawrence was doing him at all cost and he wanted Ebony just to be naïve, or so he thought.

It didn't take her long to start to play the game as well. While at work one day, Ebony was invited out to lunch with this handsome gentleman. Byron was light skin, hazel eyes and nice build. She knew that she was probably wrong to accept, but she thought that she could ask another male his perspective on the situation. At no time during the five years of being with Lawrence did Ebony ever think of cheating until Byron started showing her attention. Lawrence stopped showing her attention; it was all about him and Shawn. He accused Ebony so much of cheating and she was just a vessel for his sexual pleasure that she figured if I am constantly getting accused of it, I might as well do it!

Lawrence could sense the control he had over her slipping and he would call her at work and harass her. He would say that he knew that she was fucking around on him, which is why she never wanted to give him any. When he caught her, he was going to fuck her up. It got so bad one day that Ebony cried so much she had to leave work because she couldn't function. Ebony's supervisor never questioned what was taking place because she was such a good worker. With all the things that went on, this finally broke her down and Ebony turned to Byron for an outlet. When Byron would page her, she would return his calls. Byron didn't raise his voice to her and he showed her attention that she had missed in her husband since the day they said, "I do." The affair was short lived and only happened once. Ebony knew she was wrong, but at that moment it felt so right.

Chapter 10

Ebony's job had sent her to a training class about public speaking. While attending the class she met Lisa. Things didn't start of good, because preparing for the topic, Ebony wanted to talk about how she liked to bake and decorate cakes. Lisa outshined her and stated that she owned a bakery. Ebony and Lisa got over their differences because it was only a class. At that moment a newfound friendship was born, Lisa took Ebony under her wing. Lawrence didn't complain about them spending time together at first. Lisa shared her tricks of the trade in the business. She also let Ebony work part-time for her as an assistant. It seemed like their families had become cool, and even the husbands chatted from time to time. The girls became inseparable.

Ebony was in the midst of baking for Shawn's new daycare and ran out of flour. She called her friend Lisa and asked if she could bring over some flour and some cigarettes. Lisa arrived with the cigarettes, but only to have forgotten the main ingredient - flour. Being a good friend, she turned back around and went to retrieve the flour. At that moment, Lawrence questioned were the two women gay. He demanded to know what kind of relationship the two women shared. Ebony tried to reassure her husband that's what friends do for one another. That didn't go over so well; he cursed her out so badly that she went upstairs and cried herself to sleep. Deep in her heart she knew that he was wrong. If he would have had friends instead of always being around Ebony, then he would know better.

A couple of months had passed and it seemed like every time Lawrence's sister, Bridgette, would come to get Shawn, she would have an attitude with Ebony. Ebony didn't know why, but didn't really care. She received a phone call later that week telling her that if she didn't come and get

Shannon, then Bridgette was gonna through her ass off the balcony. Being a good samaritan, Ebony set off to see what was going on. When she arrived there, she found Shannon on the floor in the kids' room high out of her mind. She asked Bridgette what was the problem. Bridgette stated that Shannon was working at the local Amoco station where she started stealing money and getting high. She would have different men come to meet her at Bridgette's home to pick her up. She wanted Shannon out of the house immediately. All Ebony could do was shake her head. Bridgette thought that she had gotten the 411 from Shannon about Ebony. What she really didn't know was that they hadn't been around each other in years for Shannon to really know anything. Shannon had only gone on what Lawrence had fed her.

Aspiring to do the right thing, Ebony set her sights on finding a new home. Ever since returning from Guam, Ebony had her Veteran Administration paperwork to purchase a home. Since the deal didn't go through the first time, she had been finagling the bills, robbing Peter to pay Paul. They lived in a rental and it seemed that the landlord wouldn't fix anything. Spring had sprung and they couldn't open up the windows due to having no screens in the window. People would have to call first before they arrived because there was no bell. Ebony had just about had enough. This was no way to live after giving people your hard earned money.

One sunny morning she decided that this was the day. Since Lawrence was not a good manager of money, he never paid what she did any attention in that aspect. She sent Lawrence around the corner to get the number off the house that was for sale. Lawrence didn't know why Ebony had asked this of him. Ebony was a person that when she set her mind to something that is what she did. Her mind was set on purchasing a home. She stated, "Jan 1, we are moving outta here come hell or high water!" After receiving the number from Lawrence, Ebony got the ball rolling. She contacted the first realtor that seemed to have been pretty good at keeping his word. He hooked her up with a lender and to Lawrence's surprise, Ebony called off their bills out of her head. She knew what she paid every month to each person and had all her paperwork in order. Looking at about three houses, all of them were small and could not hold their furniture. Ebony had already upgraded from what Lawrence and Sheila had so it was showroom status. She finally decided to tell her realtor to take her across the street from their current residence. After stepping foot in the door, it was the exact same house and it was gonna be theirs. The extra bonus was that it had an above ground pool and a shed out back. Things went smoothly and Ebony used her VA benefit to purchase the home. Lawrence was just along for the ride, considering he and his six sisters lived in a two bedroom home with Elizabeth. He was allowed to sign the papers because he was her husband. A month later, they were painting every night and finally moved in New Year's Day. This was a great accomplishment for Ebony, something her heart had yearned for.

Getting the home in shape was not a problem. Everything was laid out the same way as it did in the last house. The only thing that was going to be different was Shawn's room. Ebony enlisted the help of Lisa. Since Lisa had cartoon characters from decorating cakes, Ebony borrowed a few pictures and made copies onto transparencies. Lawrence and Ebony painted the characters, but Lawrence really brought them to life. He was a good artist, but didn't put his skills and talent to use very often. The room looked like a professional graced it and charged an arm and a leg.

After settling in, Ebony had purchased a portrait while living in PA. She intended to wait until they purchased a home to hang it. During the course of her hanging the picture in the living room, it fell off the wall. Wouldn't you know it, it cracked down the middle! The portrait was Biblical verses about what Love is and is not. Love would never bless this new home. It would become a place of evil, hatred, and torment.

In true Ebony fashion, she decided straight off the cuff that she wanted to make this house into her home. She decided that she would first renovate the kitchen. Even though she didn't cook that often, Lawrence did, the kitchen was very dated. Ebony found a co-worker that did kitchen upgrades on the side. He didn't charge her a lot for the renovation, just required that she purchased the materials. After the renovation was complete, Lawrence upgraded the dining room to complement the kitchen. While Ebony was sleeping, he decided to use her Lowe's' card to buy some materials. When she had awakened, he started his work. One thing that she could say about him was when he did get in the mood; he was a pretty good handyman.

It seemed like every time you turned around, something else was going on with Lawrence. Now, he wanted a new vehicle, this was the third one in a couple of years! Since the purchase of the house and the kitchen renovation, Lawrence now wanted another truck. Not one for drama, she set off with him again to a dealership. Ebony was really into the Dodge Durango at the time, but the dealer was closed. The couple ventured to the Jeep dealer were Lawrence got a Cherokee. This would only pacify him for a moment. Once again not worrying about where the money was coming from, he got his wish. After the purchase of the truck, Ebony decided that there would have to be some changes to help with the bills.

After chatting with Lisa, they both decided that they needed more income. It seemed that the bakery was not pulling in enough finances to support her family as well. Being supportive girlfriends, they went to Denny's to hatch a plan. The two of them filled out job applications at Denny's, Wal-Mart, and Kmart. These companies had signs as big as day that they were hiring, but they never received a call. They finally got a gig together cleaning office buildings. Lawrence didn't complain because he was busy sitting on his ass watching cartoons with Shawn. When the paycheck came, he was the first to have his hand out. Ebony would split the extra income and give half to him and put the other half in a secret compartment of her car. After about two days, she had to give him the other half. This was not working to help them, this was helping Lawrence. Everything she did was to his benefit, but if it wasn't then it came to an end. As long as money was in his pocket, he never worried about how she got it.

Many nights after working the day job and on the second job of dumping trash - her body would ache. Lawrence didn't care; he wanted sex, sex and more sex. Whenever she didn't give in from being too tired, another argument would ensue. "You must be fucking someone else, cause you ain't doing it to me", he would say. How in the world if she was working both jobs, could she find the time? Ebony would give in, as usual, but this wasn't good either. After the initial sex, he would do it a second time. Once she would fall off to sleep and wake up, low and behold he would be downstairs watching porno. It was like he never got enough. Was he becoming a sex addict, or, was he already one?

Chapter 11

While at Lisa's house working in the bakery one day, Ebony met Ralph. Ralph was a friend to Lisa's husband. He stood about six feet tall, dark and handsome, especially for an older man. Ralph did a lot of flirting, but Ebony never thought too much of it. Since Byron, Ebony hadn't even thought about cheating again. Soon desperate times called for desperate measures! Ebony was tired of asking Vanessa to help her family. She recalled as a child Vanessa always saying, "You never know what I had to do to get what you needed. When you have a baby, you will see what I mean." It seemed like Elizabeth; Lawrence's mother never did anything but run her damn mouth. She always told Lawrence to leave his wife. She felt that her daughter-in-law was too snooty for their family. Often she told Ebony that her family was raised on love, and Ebony was raised on materialistic things.

Ebony had stopped working the part-time job because it was torture on her back. But of course Lawrence wasn't being the man he needed to be either. He was supposed to provide for his family, not the other way around. She often wondered if he was the nagging wife, since all he did was complain that she didn't love him the way he loved her and always needed money and sex.

One day while at work, she ran into Ralph. One thing led to another and Ralph propositioned her for sex. Ebony never thought that she would sell sex for money. So she viewed it as a barter. Ralph got what he wanted and her family got what they needed. One thing about Ebony, she always put Lawrence and Shawn first. Ebony met up with Ralph a few times and got a couple of dollars out of the deal. As usual, when she went home Lawrence would complain that he needed gas money. Ebony would pull the money out of her pocket and give it to him. He would state, "You holding out on money." You would have thought that he was a drug addict. He was always looking for a quick fix and needed money.

Ebony was beginning to embark on a new journey. Her tour of duty was ending and she was getting an honorable discharge from the military. She had been trying to receive a medical discharge, but to no avail. Ebony reached the decision just to get out when her time was up. Over the course of years, she could no longer participate in physical training because of breathing problems. Lawrence was ready for her to get out so that she could stay put. However; he made no provisions to become the man that he should have been and take care of his family.

Ebony lined up a job while still active in the military as a transportation clerk, but she had to let that job go. Basically, she was working on her off days which left little time for Shawn and school. She ran into her former real estate agent and he hooked her up with another agent that needed help. She took the gig because he allowed her to continue school and attend morning classes. This was gravy for Lawrence because he got to keep his eyes on her. There would be no excuse for her to go out at night.

Time had moved so quickly and the three months was finally up. Transition to civilian life was moving pretty well, because it seemed that she always was working part time somewhere. She knew that the income would be different and that her family would have to improvise on certain things. First thing she did was pulled Shawn out of daycare and placed him in the care of a person that Lisa recommended. Lawrence just went on with "he still needed this and that." Ebony was really getting disgusted with his non-chalant attitude. It seemed that as long as he had money, the house or anything else could just lapse.

The summer of 99', Elizabeth and her new husband arrived in Virginia Beach. This was the first visit that she had ever made to Lawrence's. The moment that she walked through the door, she told Lawrence that he better stay there and not leave. Ebony couldn't believe what she was hearing. She felt that for her to be so-called materialistic by her mother-in-law, why the sudden change of heart? It seemed as though whenever someone came to visit Lawrence was the perfect husband. Of course he perpetrated the fraud and became Big Willie, like he had money to give away. The only person that seemed to pick up on it was Elizabeth's husband. He provided some money for food to have a family cookout. The three sisters that lived in town and their children all attended the cookout. As usual, Lawrence needed to use Ebony's credit card to get pool cleaner. He wanted to make a statement to his mother that he had arrived. Ebony was glad when his family left, she didn't have to act like she liked them. The coolest person out the bunch was Elizabeth's husband. Maybe he was used to them mooching off of people, but she wasn't.

Chapter 12

Ebony had begun to use her grant and student loan money to pay bills. The real estate job didn't last long, only three months. After all the hard work she had done for the agent, he began to bounce payroll checks. After arriving to work from class, he told her that today would be her last day. He could no longer afford her on the payroll. Ebony didn't wait that long, she gathered her things and left immediately. Her thought was to go home and plan out a strategy to make ends meet. After working since the age of fourteen, she considered applying for unemployment. This was an entitlement Ebony felt she deserved.

First thing the next morning Ebony darted out the door after dropping Shawn off at the sitters. She was on her way to file for unemployment. Once she got down there, it seemed that the lines were long and people were not friendly at all. After the initial paperwork, she began to look for jobs that would coincide with her morning classes. The people at the agency told her that it would take two weeks for her to start drawing a check, but she would have to be actively looking for a job. Ebony really wasn't in a hurry to start work again, it seemed like she had been working constantly. This would be her break and a chance to continue the current semester.

The following week she received a letter stating that her claim was being denied. Ebony being the business person that she was went to the office in a fury. She had encountered a worker there that tried to explain that her line of work was only a 9-5 shift. That meant that she could obtain viable employment, but since she was currently in school in the mornings that was her own fault. Ebony really wasn't one to go off, but she felt that she had worked all her life and it wasn't their damn money. She deserved her fair share as well. She looked the clerk in the eye and leaned over the counter and stated "How do you tell your child that is hungry that you can't feed him?" As one tear escaped her eye, the clerk advised Mrs. Richmond to go in the bathroom and get herself together. When Ebony arrived back to the counter, the clerk told her that she would have a check within a couple of days.

Things were beginning to fall on hard times. She couldn't pay the babysitter and started sending food and drinks for the whole family to pay for the couple of days that Shawn went there. Ebony felt like she couldn't afford to pay for the services rendered, but she could charge food on her credit card to help feed her child and whoever else that lived at the babysitter's. In this whole matter, Lawrence left it up to his wife to handle everything, as long as he had his cigarettes and gas money.

The clerk took care of Ebony and she finally started receiving checks. Ebony milked it until the semester was over. Once the semester was over, she could actively seek employment. Virginia Employment Commission sent her on a job interview at a company. The position Ebony had applied for was filled in house. The manager offered her the receptionist position. Ebony knew deep down, she didn't want it. She had purposely gone on the interview without stockings, and wearing sandals but to her surprise was hired despite it all. Ebony could not decline it, because the Employment Commission definitely would stop her checks. Things were beginning to fall in place with the babysitter.

The job didn't last long because the person training Ebony tried to talk to her like a child. Ebony explained to the supervisor that she had spent half of this young girl's life in the military and she was not going to stand for it. The supervisor flat out told Ebony that she would be let go before the young girl. His words came true because a day later, they marched Ebony right out of the building. Once again back to the Employment Commission, Ebony went. While there she hooked up with a nice clerk. This lady told Ebony to type up an application because the agency was hiring. Ebony had been there so much, she was hired. It was only part-time but it was an opening to get a full time state government position.

Being the aspiring person that she was, Ebony wanted more out of life. The job was great because it provided income, but she really didn't do much. Her supervisor would not let her do her homework while at work, so she resorted to investigating serial killers. She wanted to see what made them tick and to study their minds. Maybe she had one at home living with her and didn't know it.

Her stay at the Employment Commission was short lived, only four months. Ebony had taken a job with Portsmouth Probation and Parole. Trying to find out how the system works, it was going to be best to look at it from all angles. Ebony remembered her last day at the Employment office, telling her fellow co-workers, "Don't be surprised if you see me as a judge one day."

While on her journey with a new job, Ebony began to work hard to learn all that she could. Once again tragedy would interfere. Lawrence got his orders to transfer to New Orleans. Ebony was not happy with the situation, because he now wanted to uproot the family there. After vacationing there, Ebony thought that it was a waste of time. She did research and found that the school system sucked and the jobs didn't pay well. She was trying to compromise the best she could. Since they had just moved into their home, why would she want to move? Ebony had invested money into this home and did major renovations. Why give up a place to go to another city that she did not care for?

Ebony was fighting a losing battle; she tried to weigh the pros and cons of the situation. Lawrence was not making it any easier. Being in the military like he was, he should have known that when it was time to go, it was time. She told him that she did not come with his sea bag and that he needed to just go by himself. He was only going to be there for two years. There would be no use in uprooting the family just for two years. She was in school, Shawn was getting ready to go to kindergarten and they had just brought the house. All hell broke out because at this point, Lawrence deemed that Ebony did not love him. The plan was settled, Ebony stuck to her guns.

Ebony had taken a couple of days off her job to help Lawrence drive to New Orleans. That way Shawn could ride and take a trip back by plane. Ebony wanted her son to explore all the things in life that she had and more. During the course of their travels, they stopped in "Hot-lanta." Lawrence's older sister, Cathy and her family now lived there. Since Ebony had never been, she found Atlanta to be exciting. The town was gorgeous and she decided that she could live there. Lawrence had been stationed there before and decided to take his wife on a tour. The homes were beautiful and the people were really friendly. They decided to go to an open house. Ebony told Lawrence that if he got stationed there, then and only then, would she move and sell the property in Virginia. This was more viable and had better living conditions than New Orleans, she thought.

Ebony didn't know what it was about her husband, but it seemed like every damn time he got around his family he was someone different.

Granted Ebony didn't go anywhere without paying her way, but she thought that family was supposed to help out in a crisis? She didn't have a problem buying and helping prepare food. One night, the adults decided to hang out and see Atlanta nightlife. Dinner and a strip club would do. While at dinner, Lawrence told his sister and her husband that he had the meal. For the life of Ebony, she couldn't understand it. Knowing that they had been struggling: gas for driving there, plane fare for her and the baby, and then bills when she got home. This was really draining her pockets. Cathy's husband decided that he would get the entrance into the strip club. This would sort of be an even trade. This wasn't the first strip club that the Richmond's had been to together. As usual, Lawrence acted like he was not interested. Of course if Ebony was not there, he would have enjoyed himself. Ebony really liked going, she thought that she would learn new moves to keep her husband interested in her. This was her logic, but Lawrence's was that she was gay.

The family made it to New Orleans safe and sound. Ebony and Shawn stayed two days at the Navy Lodge. Lawrence and Ebony had made a decision that Lawrence should come home at least once a month, twice if they could afford it. Getting back on her grind, Ebony had a new outlook. She had to provide for Shawn, the house, the dogs, juggle school full-time and work full-time. It was gonna be task but she was up to the challenge. She had no choice; black women had been doing it for years.

Not long after getting the job, Ebony had to go away for three days of training. Vanessa and Leroy made their way down to care for Shawn, the house, and the dogs. She did not want to let her parents know that she didn't have any money. She did the best she could while there. This was a learning experience for her. She was so use to taking care of everyone else that she went without for far too long. After returning back and getting settled back into things, Ebony met a co-worker named Nate. Nate reminded her so much of her stepfather, a sharp dresser and smelled good. Nate had taken a liking to Ebony also. Ebony was good at her job and everyone knew that if they wanted something done quick, give it to her. Nate began to slide a lot of work her way and in turn he began to mentor her about staying in college. She became the multi-tasker, juggling work, homework and chatting with Lawrence all on the job's computer.

The shit was getting thick and he wasn't even gone a month. Via the internet while at work, he started saying that she was cheating. Ebony did everything in her power to just let it go, thinking that her husband was just missing home. To add more pressure, I guess he had talked to Elizabeth.

She called Ebony and wanted to know, "Why she didn't go to New Orleans with her husband?" Instead of asking could she help them out in anyway, if Shawn needed milk or whatever, she came with bullshit. Ebony had taken all she could take. She politely told her mother-in-law that if she was concerned, she should move down there with him.

After about two months, Lawrence made the journey home for a visit. While there, Ebony tried to show him as much love and affection as she could. She had a major test coming up, but he didn't want to hear of it. If the quality time wasn't about him, then she could forget it. She ended up flunking her test and to make matters worst, Lawrence had received a speeding ticket. How on earth would they pay for it? Things were going down hill, so once again Ebony called her mother. Vanessa provided the money to pay for the ticket.

It had been a hard task but Ebony was finally graduating with her Associates Degree in June. She didn't want Lawrence to attend the graduation because he had tried hindering the process. He did everything in his power to try to break her concentration. Vanessa and Leroy were the first to arrive, followed by Barbara and Ebony's aunt. The graduation was smooth and the best part about it was that Ebony had Nate there also. Nate had pushed Ebony to continue her studies and had bought some of her textbooks.

Afterwards the family, including Nate went to Ruby Tuesday's to celebrate. Barbara and her daughter looked at Nate strangely. Vanessa and Leroy already knew the deal. They had spent many occasions in Virginia when the four of them would hang out together. Ebony's parents knew her all too well. There was nothing that she did that they didn't know about. Nate was Ebony's sugar daddy. He stepped up to the plate and helped provide for Shawn and her. Lawrence was never sending any money, but always needing it. Ebony always loved a man that reminded her of her step father. Nate was just that, older and more mature. He never saw Ebony or her child without.

Chapter 13

She couldn't take it anymore. Ebony moved into the guest bedroom. But before she did, this is what transpired. See while Ebony and Shawn was in Baltimore, Lawrence slept with her girlfriend, Keyshawna. Keyshawna was Ebony's roommate while they were stationed in Guam. The two became inseparable at a time. They even went and got co-signing gold in their mouths alike. When Keyshawna got married, Ebony and Lawrence drove all they way to Ohio for the wedding. She became Keyshawna's child godmother. Keyshawana did the same when Ebony got married. She was there. The girls shared everything from clothing to men sometimes. This was the only relationship Ebony had from her Navy days to hold onto.

Usually he would call to check on her twenty times, but not this time. When Ebony and Shawn arrived home, she noticed Lawrence drawers on the floor beside the bed. The bed was a mess. Ebony looked at the caller id. She saw that Keyshawna had called around 2:30 in the morning.

Ebony started putting two and two together. Keyshawna knew Ebony had gone to take Shawn to see her real father. When she asked Lawrence about it, the lies begin to flow out of his damn mouth. "She called to let me know she made it home safely." Ebony thought to herself – what the fuck for! The next shocker told her why. Ebony went into their on-suite bathroom. She found a long piece of black hair on the sink. Last time she checked, due to all the stress and her hair falling out, she had orange short curly hair. Lawrence didn't even have the decency to change the sheets. "What a fucking pig!"

It had been about a week now that she was in the other room. Ebony just couldn't take all the lying and deceiving that was going on in the house. Deep down inside all she really wanted was to "Be Happy" like Mary J. Blige said.

She was in her room studying and minding her own business, when the door flew off the hinges. What the fuck! Lawrence had kicked the door in just to argue about her not having sex with him. Ebony was fed up with the bullshit and had enough. She had just about taken all that she could from him. When the word bitch flew out of his mouth, Ebony lost it. She snapped, cracked and popped that ass in the mouth! The two began to fight and Lawrence pushed Ebony into the wall. The throbbing pain in her back would not subside, but this time she continued to fight for her life.

The altercation moved downstairs, because Shawn was now in his room posted in a corner scared to death. Lawrence pushed her so hard, her body slammed against the refrigerator door. As she managed to get to her feet, she grabbed a frying pan. She was going for the first thing she could get to. He snatched it out of her hands and acted as if he was going to hit her with it. As she began to back away he pushed her harder into the kitchen island. It rocked her body so hard that the whole island moved. (This island held pots and pans and was not on wheels.)

Lawrence had Ebony by the throat; she was back peddling trying to reach for anything on the kitchen counter. She was actually going for the butcher block with the knives in it. She couldn't quite reach it. His hands finally gave way and Ebony ran for the phone. In all the years of abuse, she never once fought back or called the police. But this time she had too.

When the officers arrived, one questioned Lawrence and the other Ebony. The officer could clearly see the bruises that began to appear around her shoulders and neck. Lawrence was good at fooling everyone. The smooth talking person that he was, he did just that with the officers. The next thing Ebony knew, she was being read her rights. The officer told her that she could either do it the easy way or the hard way. Ebony had now worked at the Chesapeake Police Department for about a year, and asked could she please put on some clothes. All she had on was a negligee since she had just gotten out of the shower. He told her that she was not allowed to go back upstairs. She politely asked could she make a call. She called Nate so that he could inform her parents. The whole time, Lawrence had this smug grin on his face. He had told the officers, that she pulled a butcher's knife on him and tried to stab him.

Before she was lead out the door, here comes Keyshawna. She ran upstairs to get a shirt and a skirt for Ebony. Ebony asked if she could leave without handcuffs since she worked at the police department. This asshole was aggorant and stated "No." "Put your hands behind your back." By this time, the neighbors began to gather in front of Ebony's house. Shawn was crying hysterically as his mother was being lead outside in handcuffs.

Being handcuffed like a hardened criminal, Ebony couldn't even bring herself to cry. All she could do was keep her head held high as she was being placed into the cruiser. During the ride to jail, God spoke to Ebony, "Enough is enough." After arriving to be process, the magistrate looked at Ebony funny. She went over the charges with Ebony, but couldn't for the life of her figure out what was going on. Ebony explained what had happened. She told the magistrate that she had never been in trouble a day in her life and that she was defending herself. The magistrate could see the sincerity in her eyes that she let her go on her own recognizance.

Before she could be released they had her sit down to cool off. Ebony knew that she would have peace, as soon as he left to go back to New Orleans in the morning with Shawn. This would give her sometime to think over how she could get out of this dangerous situation. After being booked and charged and then fingerprinted, they finally released her. The only number that Ebony knew off the bat was Keyshawna's.

As Ebony limped up the dark and deserted roadway, no one would even stop to help her. Not even a police. She continued to endure the pain in her body as she limped towards home. Even Lawrence with his simple ass would not even come and get her. It seemed like it was an eternity, but it had only been about fifteen minutes. As she ventured further, she could see lights. Finally Keyshawna showed up, Ebony wanted to say, "You fake-ass bitch". She held her tongue just to accept the ride only a few blocks away from her house.

After arriving home, all she could think of was going to sleep. However; she called her mother to let her know that she was fine. Vanessa was very disappointed to know that Nate had to call her and not Lawrence. Vanessa began to see the true colors of Lawrence now. How could he let his wife get arrested and not try to do anything to help her out?

The following morning as Ebony awoke, Lawrence and Shawn were gone. Vanessa had called and told her daughter that she had to move. If she didn't, she was coming for her. Ebony assured her mother that she would do something, but she wasn't sure what or how. The next day while driving to work, every record that played on the radio told Ebony that she could began again. At that moment, her soul had become uplifted and she truly believed that God was telling her something.

Ebony got up the nerve to ask a co-worker for help. After work the two drove to some apartment complexes. Ebony didn't know how she would be able to afford rent. She put in a couple of applications, but there were no openings for a while. Ebony called her mother for advice. She knew deep down inside she needed to get away from this man.

After returning home that night, Ebony found a pamphlet that was laid on the counter that the police gave Lawrence. As she read it, it was pertaining to domestic violence. Ebony reached for the phone and made the call. The lady on the other end assured Ebony that everything was confidential and that they had a shelter and women's group meetings every Thursday night. This was something Ebony needed and wanted to try. Was there other people going through similar situations just like her?

In her heart she was waiting for Nate to rescue her. He had her back on every situation and they had been seeing each other for over a year now. Two weeks had passed and he finally wanted her to move in with him. Nate had a four bedroom house in Hampton and it was more than enough room for Ebony. Nate told her that he needed time to digest the situation. She didn't want to hear it, because all the fun they had going places and making passionate love together, he should have done something sooner. Ebony passed up on the offer because she felt like he should have told her that the day she came from jail.

Ebony had read in the paper that she could get a divorce for five hundred dollars. She didn't have that kind of money, due to Lawrence. She didn't have to ask twice, her mother was all over it. The money was there within three days. Ebony had begun the process for divorce. As she spoke with the attorney, he stated that she could be divorced within a week. He knew a judge that was cool with him and could squeeze her on the docket. Ebony was ecstatic. She forwarded the money and paperwork to the lawyer.

All good things come to a close. Ebony didn't know how Lawrence and Shawn got to the airport and hadn't heard from them while they were gone. She received a call that they were stuck in Dulles and needed a ride. She felt as though his girlfriend or Keyshawna should have gone to get them. He didn't bother to help get her from jail. If she had a mean streak in her body, she would have left him. Ebony was not that kind of person, but she was feeling that way. Thinking mostly of her baby, she set off for the journey to retrieve the two.

The ride was a rocky one; she encountered thunder storms and pouring rain. Once she arrived, Lawrence really didn't say anything to her. He had a box in his hands from Victoria Secrets. All Ebony could think of, was that it was for someone else. The only reason he was giving it to her was due to having to pick his stupid ass up. They rode in total silence.

Sitting at the kitchen counter debating to go to group meeting, something kept tugging at Ebony's heart. Lawrence opened up his dumb mouth and was like, "Why don't you go?" It was as if he wanted her to get out the house, but something else awaited her there. She needed her school paper looked over and the person that was going to help would be there. As she arrived, there was a new face amongst the crowd. The women gathered around in a circle and commence to telling their stories. Ebony noticed this young lady crying her eyes out. She never spoke, just cried. She was the prettiest girl, but she had on all this makeup that was not blended in and a horrible wig. Ebony overlooked it because at that point, they all were there for one reason or another. The session had ended and as some stragglers stayed, Ebony approached the group looking for help that she needed. A small voice spoke up and said, "I can help you with your paper." The girl that cried the whole session name was Gwen.

Gwen and Ebony became real close friends. Ebony dwelled on Gwen's problems to get away from her own. The two gave each other something that they needed. Ebony took time to show Gwen how to apply her makeup and asked why she wore wigs all the time. When Gwen took it off, her hair was down her back. As Ebony began to focus on upgrading Gwen, Gwen in turn helped Ebony with her schooling. Gwen was a genius, which was not given enough credit by her own husband. This became their special bond with one another.

The Richmond's was just co-habituating in the house at this point. The mail had finally come, and it was the divorce papers. While sitting at the dining room table, Ebony handed them for Lawrence to sign. He cried like a baby, "Please don't do this, make love to me." Ebony thought he was crazy because if she did sleep with him, they couldn't get divorced. Last time she checked, he wasn't in love with her. He only used her for sexual gratification and money. He promised her with all his might that he would change, just don't divorce him.

Ebony wanted to have faith in this man and believe his words. Apart of her was willing to accept it, and the other part wanted to run for the hills. Against her better judgment, Ebony called the lawyer. She pleaded with the lawyer not to go through with it. He could keep the full payment. Two days later as Ebony was preparing to go to church, Lawrence started talking smart. This puzzled her because of what she had just done. "Bitch, ain't nobody tell you not to get divorced", he stated. At that moment, she felt like a complete and uttered fool. All she could do was leave for church and cry in the car. She thought that she just threw her mother's money out the window.

A week later, Lawrence returned back to New Orleans. Ebony was glad that his ass was gone. It seemed so much peaceful in the house, with her and Shawn. How could she teach her son the right things, if he was witnessing an abusive situation? During Lawrence's time away, it seemed that Ebony was even more so motivated to finish school.

She needed a much need break, so one night while out with Lauren, a member of the church ministry. They decided to go to the Hampton Coliseum to see Ebony's favorite group, Maze featuring Frankie Beverly. The show was off the hook and she was really enjoying herself. Lawrence couldn't interfere because he was in New Orleans. After the show, the girls weren't in a hurry to rush home. Shawn was over his god brother's house for the night. So they decided a little while longer wouldn't hurt. The two ran across this little club down in Norfolk. While there Lawrence kept calling Ebony to see where she was and when she was going home. Ebony tried to ease his mind by stating in a few. Once she got there, they could have phone sex.

The club was really crowded and the music was nice. They were having a Mardi gras event, giving away beads. The ladies had a couple of drinks and danced by themselves. Ebony looked up and a group of young looking thugs entered the club. This was the girls cue to leave. As they left the dance floor to get their belongings to exit, one of the dudes approached Ebony. She had to admit he was a fine tenderoni. He stated that his name was Kim and why was she leaving; him and his boys had just gotten there. Jokingly she told Kim, that she was probably old enough to be his mother. He had to be about nineteen in her mind. Kim was light-skinned with a baby face, naturally curly hair and had a northern accent. She learned that he was from New York and had that swagger. It seemed like he had an answer for everything she threw his way. He was smooth and said age is nothing but a number. Ebony started blushing from ear to ear because he was fine as hell. She thought to herself, "Why in the world a young man would try to pull an older woman?" Come to find out, he was only six years younger than Ebony. She told him that she had to go and that she was married. Kim with his soft sexy voice stated, "Here is my number, if you're happy discard it, if you are not happy - I'm tryin to holla." Once the girls got outside Ebony looked at Lauren and said let me throw this number away. Lauren looked back like - girl he was fine, do you really want to! With much debate, Ebony pocketed the number and proceeded home to call her husband.

After getting settled in, she called Lawrence. It was every bit of one in the morning and he never answered his phone. She finally gave up and went to bed. The next morning she tried again with no luck. At that time she phoned his sister that he was staying with. She told Ebony that Lawrence had left two hours ago and said that he would be right back. Ebony left a message for him to call her, but he never did. If the shoe was on the other foot, he would have pitched a bitch. Ebony had something for that; it was called "Kim." She reached into her pocket and pulled out the number. Contemplating more on calling then not, she reached for the phone. After the initial ring, Ebony decided that she should not do this. Apart of her wanted to because of all that Lawrence had put her through, but the other half was trying to be a good wife and mother. Her head was spinning over the decision, but the brother was too damn fine and he was interested in her. The phone rang two times and Kim answered the phone. Straight off the bat, he knew who she was. Most men try to pick up many women and can't place where they met you at. In her book that meant that he hadn't forgotten her. The two chatted for about an hour. Kim wanted to see Ebony again. Ebony explained her circumstances and he was down for whatever.

Lawrence finally called that night with some bullshit excuse that he went fishing. He had been using that line on Ebony for a minute, since he had been stationed in New Orleans. Ebony decided to do some investigating. While Shawn was upstairs playing in his room, she set down at the computer. Each person had only one email account, so she thought. After digging and playing with passwords, Ebony discovered that Lawrence had three different accounts. Upon cracking the code to the second one, it was loaded with emails and pictures of a young female. This person was expressing to Lawrence how he made her feel and that she would see him later. She had also sent him six nude pictures of herself sprawled out in front of a fireplace.

Ebony had just about had enough. She thought, "Two could play that game!" She wasn't happy since the wedding, really. But looking back on it, she always tried to save face because of her mother. Ebony thought about all the money her mother had spent for that wedding. She didn't want it to look like she was a failure and leave her husband. But if he was gonna cheat and dog her, then she would find comfort in someone else's arms.

Chapter 14

For the past year, she had been working full-time, going to school full-time and taking care of the family. She had always supported the family with two jobs, or whatever she had to do to get money. Now he was down in New Orleans and she was supporting him down there. Lawrence had claimed to have a job at the local supermarket, but Ebony never received a dime to help out with anything. To her, the money must have gone to Miss Luscious that was spread eagle wide for him.

Taking a break from the day to day grind, Ebony wanted some quality time to herself. She enlisted the help of Gwen to watch Shawn. Kim had talked to her earlier that day and they decided to meet on base. They went to the movies and then to Applebee's. Damn, he was finer than she remembered. The club was dark, but from what she had seen, he was handsome. Just sitting across the table from him, it was like she was out of her league. Ebony really hadn't dated a light-skinned dude in her life, besides Byron. And that was just a one time deal. During their talk, Ebony didn't disclose all that was going on within her marriage. Kim could sense that it was more to it than she let on, but he didn't want to rush her. He figured she would open up eventually, he had time. The evening relieved her mind and she went home just thinking about all the two had discussed. It was as if Lawrence could sense something was going on because he called. Boy did he know how to fuck up a good moment. Ebony didn't let that distract her.

Kim and Ebony began to chat everyday and finally he decided that he wanted to meet Ebony at the Navy Lodge. He had been preparing all week to get a room off base. Ebony was down for it as well. It had been a good lil minute since a man and a younger man at that, wanted quality time with her. She set off to cook Kim his favorite meal. Shawn was spending the weekend at his god bother's house, so that freed Ebony up. Ebony went to the supermarket and got all the food that Kim wanted for his dinner. It was good to cook for someone that really was appreciative. She got on the grill and cooked spare ribs, made baked macaroni and cheese, and fried cabbage. Ebony was really feeling good and got herself all dolled up. Once she met Kim at the Navy Lodge, she had little butterflies in the pit of her stomach. She knew what she was going to do when she got there, but it still felt a lil' awkward. The two laid on the bed and Ebony fed her new man. After eating and watching television for a few, they both knew what was about to go down. Things moved slowly at first, but once the two found their rhythms their bodies intertwined like it was meant to be. The feeling was so different that Ebony couldn't describe it. Their lovemaking session went on for hours til Ebony received a call. The call was that Lawrence had returned home unexpectedly. It was as if Lawrence always knew how to put a damper on things.

Gwen called, "He left me and the children!" Ebony was glad in a way, but needed to be there for her girl. Gwen explained that her family was on their way from North Carolina to move her home. Ebony was heartbroken. Someone that had her back was leaving her. Who would distract her other than Kim to take away her problems now?

Lawrence had somehow convinced his new command in New Orleans that he needed to come home due to hardship on the family. The Navy gave him temporary orders to Oceana. He hadn't been home long before things began to unravel. This just made Ebony see Kim more often. He made her feel good about herself in everyway, the way her husband was suppose to.

Lawrence began seeing a co-worker on his job. Ebony could spot the sudden change in his attitude. Whenever Lawrence was dealing with another woman, the fights with Ebony would become more intense. He began breaking up shit in the house. While doing so, Lawrence would growl like a lion and clinch his fist. His fist would go straight through the dining room wall. This would intensify, until he moved next to the furniture. All Ebony could do was shake her head. She had paid a pretty penny for what they had. You could tell when a mutha fucka wasn't use to shit. This was probably the best shit he ever had in his life.

All the stress, arguing, and fighting was beginning to take a toll on her body. Ebony was vomiting up her own bile, lost a tremendous amount of weight, and her hair was beginning to fall out. She had lost seven dress sizes. Vanessa could sense that her daughter was beginning to lose her mind. Vanessa enlisted Barbara to go to Virginia for an intervention. Barbara's arrival was sort of a wake up call for the couple. Ebony wanted to just let loose and tell her grandmother everything. Lawrence put on his charm, like the couple was fine. Only when company came over was he on his best behavior. He went to bed when Ebony went; trying to act like this was the norm. Lawrence's appearance was that of a loving husband, but deep down he was hell on wheels. Barbara started to sense that everything was not what it appeared to be.

Ebony took her grandmother to her church's revival. During the services, Ebony walked to the front in desperate need of prayer. However; she did not notice that Barbara was behind her. The good reverend called out her issue and explained that Ebony needed to get out of bondage. She knew exactly what she needed to do, but could she? Ebony herself was caught up in what people thought of her. Lawrence didn't help the matter at all. He was like the lion just waiting to devour his prey. The old saying is that misery loves company and that is what he liked in the home. There was no peace and no rest.

Shawn was beginning to feel the effects of this bad relationship. He began to act out and only wanted his dad because his dad was his friend. Ebony had begun to withdraw from her son. Although she loved him dearly, his father was brainwashing him. Lawrence had started taking Shawn over his new girlfriend's house. When Shawn would arrive home, he would say things like "he wished he had a new mother." This cut Ebony like a knife. All the degrading stuff that she had endured to make sure her family flourished was in vain. Lawrence would just smile and tell Ebony, "He can say what he wants to say." In all the years Ebony was growing up, the taste would be slapped out of your mouth if she ever told her mother something like that. Ebony was losing her child to this monster that came from a line of abusers. She just kept praying that Shawn did not turn out like his father.

All the outrageous insults Lawrence would give to Ebony, she began to take them all in stride. Ebony just wanted peace. She found that in Kim. One night Ebony and Kim had just left dinner and a movie. She had planned on seeing him later that week. Her mind was on cloud nine when she returned home. After entering the house and trying to check on Shawn, Lawrence started in. Ebony just redialed her cell phone to let the other person listen. As she raised the phone to her ear, Kim stated get some clothes and come and get me. Lawrence was still cursing her out as she walked upstairs. Ebony gladly got some clean clothes and got the fuck out of there. Since Gwen was gone, she had nowhere to run-but to Kim's arms.

Vanessa had threatened her daughter to leave. "If you don't move, I will get a U-haul and come and bring your ass home." Ebony didn't want to return back to Baltimore. She felt like she had a better life in Virginia. Her fear was leaving and starting all over again. On the other hand, she knew that her mother was serious. The following day, Ebony set out to find a place of her own. With all the bills in her name, she wondered how in God's name she would be able to afford rent. She traveled to some less desirable neighborhoods of Norfolk, Virginia Beach, and Chesapeake. It didn't take her long; she found a place in Chesapeake.

While at this apartment complex, Ebony was sharing her story with the leasing agent. She told her that she had to leave her husband due to domestic violence. The agent explained to Ebony that it was a fee that needed to be paid by money order. Ebony only carried her checkbook, but told the agent she would return in a few minutes. Upon returning, a man was there also applying for an apartment. He had overheard Ebony's story and decided to give up his spot, so that she could move within the next week. She was so grateful to this complete stranger. When she arrived at the apartment, she couldn't place at first where she remembered it from. It flashed really quickly and it came to mind. During off work hours, Ebony had been going on ride alongs with the Police Department. The apartment over from the building she was being showed had been broken into. This scared her a little, but was glad in a way that the guy gave up his apartment. This particular one did not have a patio like the one that had been broken into. Ebony signed the lease and was to move in next week.

She was so excited that she was gonna be free, but in the back of her mind was how she was going to pay the bills. During the evening time after picking up Shawn, Ebony would go to Big Lots and purchase dishes and towels for her new apartment. She started storing them in the trunk of her car. It was only a couple of more days until she made her escape. Ebony enlisted the help of some of her friends at the women's shelter. Friday would be the day that she would make her escape.

It was only four days til Christmas when Ebony decided it was time to go. She called Shawn in the room and tried to explain that she was going to allow him to open up at least two of his presents. Shawn grabbed his mom by the hand and proceeded downstairs to the family room. Lawrence looked at the two in amazement. He asked Ebony what was going on. "I am just tired and I want Shawn to open up at least two of his presents" she said. She didn't think that he got it, which was cool with her. After Shawn was excited about opening the two gifts, Ebony decided to go back upstairs and get some rest.

The big day! Friday morning Ebony arose and got dress. Before she left out the door she kissed Shawn goodbye. Lawrence just rolled his eyes at her. What he did not notice, was Ebony had the same clothes on she wore to work on Tuesday. This should have been a clue to him, because she never wore the same thing twice, hardly ever. She took the fifteen minute drive to her new apartment, received the keys and got to work. Ebony started unloading all the items she had stored in her car. After that, she began to clean the kitchen and the bathroom.

Once she thought that Lawrence and Shawn had gone, she doubled back to the house. Tamara had hired Two Men and a Truck to help her with the heavy furniture. As they arrived, her friends had their cars packed with items also. It didn't take them but only forty-five minutes to clear out the entire downstairs. She took the living room, dining room and guest bedroom furniture. The entertainment center was too big to fit in the apartment or she would have stripped that too. Ebony thought, "My name is on all this shit and he fucked up everything. He expects me to leave with nothing. I am eating peanut butter and jelly sandwiches and buying him cigarettes. He got a nerve to buy her lunch everyday. Now ain't that a bitch!"

The day was really going smoothly; she had gotten everything that she wanted out of the house. Ebony was a neat freak, so all her stuff was put away as soon as she got everything into the apartment. Finally it was peace and quite. She had already had her phone and lights cut on, and cable was just a week a way. Ebony figured she could watch movies til then. The first person she called was her mother to let her know that she was safe. She started to turn her cell phone off, but before she could it rang and Lawrence was on the other end. Ebony asked him not to pick Shawn up yet, to go home first. Lawrence had already stated that he had Shawn with him. All Ebony could say was "OK". She wondered in the back of her mind, why he was calling her anyway. This was not his norm when he had another woman. He cared less for Ebony and it showed. After hanging up the phone, she turned it off. Lawrence was about to get the shock of his life.

Rest sweet rest. It never felt so good to take a long hot bath and get a peaceful nights rest. Before going to bed, she did however check her messages. "Bitch, you were fucking dead wrong. No wonder you didn't want me to pick up Shawn yet. Fuck you bitch; I can't stand your ass anyway." Lawrence voice glared through the phone. "Who had the last laugh?" Ebony thought.

Being gone for only a month Ebony was pretty happy with her life. Kim was staying there with her. It was different than with Lawrence. The two hung out at clubs together and Kim was open to Ebony wearing whatever she wanted. "I know who you're going home with", he would say. Kim didn't mind if men looked at his woman, because that meant he had something special.

Ebony always compared the two in the back of her mind. She had fun with Kim, but it seemed that she was scared that he would leave her for a younger, more beautiful woman. Since Vanessa had threatened her daughter to move, she decided to come down and see how things were going. Vanessa arrived at her daughter's place and was glad that she was alright. The only problem she ran into was that she was not used to Kim. With Lawrence, Vanessa could move around freely and go in her daughter's room. Don't get it twisted!!!!! Vanessa was the type of person that said what was on her mind.

The three of them sat down and ate dinner together and chatted. This eased her mind a bit. Vanessa and Ebony had planned on going to church, and Kim didn't want to be excluded. He went to the mall and brought some dress slacks, since he was used to wearing jeans only. Sunday morning the three ventured off to church. From there Vanessa really got a good vibe from Kim. It seemed like he was not trying to throw shade at her like Lawrence. Vanessa could see that for once her daughter laughed and smiled, and it wasn't a charade she was playing.

The new couple decided to drive Vanessa home and spend the day just chatting and getting to know one another better. During the drive, for some reason, Vanessa blurted out, "ya'll would have pretty kids." Kim and Ebony just looked at one another because Kim had just paid for Ebony to have an abortion.

After arriving in Baltimore, Kim first got a chance to met Barbara. Barbara smiled from ear to ear and wanted to know how old this young man was. She whispered in Ebony's ear, "he is cute, but looks like a baby." Ebony explained to her grandmother that for once, in a long time, she was happy. Ebony's cousin, Miko had arrived to take Barbara to lunch. This is something that she did every Monday. While pulling up, she saw Ebony outside. Once making it into the house and she saw Kim, she told Ebony she was going to have her locked up for child molestation. Both of the girls laughed. The whole group went to a restaurant in Timonium. The family had fifty and one questions for Kim. He took them all in stride and was calm and mild mannered. The couple returned home and things got back to normal.

Ebony went to work just smiling. Things seemed to be going good in her life since she had left Lawrence. As usual Lawrence decided that he had another plan in the works for Ebony. She had left him high and dry and he wasn't gonna go for it. What could break her at this point- nothing, she believed. Until she got a call that day from the Sheriff's office. The sheriff told Ebony that he was downstairs and needed to serve her with papers. He didn't want to impose on her while she was at work, but wanted to do it quietly and swiftly. He asked her was there a way for her to come downstairs, so that her co-workers didn't see. Ebony met him outside and thanked him for being so kind. She knew that he was only doing his job.

Wouldn't you know that it was court documents for custody of Shawn! The smile and happiness she had was snatched from her. Why couldn't this man just leave her alone she thought? He had his woman, but that wasn't enough. She couldn't be happy. He always wanted her to be miserable.

The court date was fast approaching and it seemed as if Kim was in his own little world. He decided that he was going home for the weekend. Ebony pleaded with him to go, she really needed to go and clear her head. Kim stated that this was not a good time to go, but he would surely take her the next time around.

As Ebony took the day off of work to go to court, she tried to talk some sense into Lawrence. Whatever she said, it went in one ear and out the other. They settled on mediation before making the final decision. Ebony asked Lawrence if she could keep Shawn that weekend. He reluctantly agreed. She figured since Kim was going away, this would be the opportunity to have Shawn over.

Ebony never let Shawn see her with anyone except for his father. She figured her mother didn't have different men around and she wouldn't either. After the Richmond's left the courthouse, Lawrence persuaded Ebony to come to the house to talk about filing that year's taxes. Ebony being naive went. It seemed as if one thing lead to another and Lawrence was having sex with Ebony for the good times. Afterwards, he stated that she could come pick Shawn up that Friday night. When she got home, she felt a little guilty that she had just slept with her so- called husband. Kim didn't notice anything different; it wasn't as if the two of them was getting down like that. The sex with them came to a crawl after she got pregnant and had the abortion due to his wishes. In the back of Ebony's mind, all she could think about was seeing her son on Friday. She thought that she would call to talk to Shawn. The phone just rang off the hook with no answer. She even called Lawrence's phone and no answer there either.

The following day she did the same, with no such luck. Finally Friday came and after calling repeatedly, Ebony finally called Shawn's school. The secretary first told Ebony that Shawn was in class, and then an administrator gave her the shock of her life - Shawn had been pulled out of school with transfer papers to New Orleans. The air had been grabbed from her lungs. She started hyperventilating and couldn't breathe. Ebony had to leave work; she just couldn't take it anymore.

When she arrived home, it seemed like she cried and couldn't stop. Shortly thereafter, Kim came to get his clothes for his trip to New York. Ebony tried to make him stay with her. She needed him at this time in her life. Once again Kim was like he had to go; he left her high and dry. The girl was really losing her mind at this point.

Completely calming down from the situation, she knew she had to get herself together. She wasn't going to let this die. Always being nice to him, and this how his fucking ass treated her. Believing that he would be a man of his word, everything he said was a fucking lie. In order for her to get it together, Ebony became like a private investigator. First she called the mediation people at the courts, no one could help her. Then she tried calling Lawrence again to no avail. She had cracked his code to his phone again, and found a message on there. The message was from his girlfriend stating that she was going over the house later to let the dogs out. Hell naw Ebony thought, not in this lifetime. Ebony got on the phone with a locksmith that met her at the house. She had the locks changed on the door, not Lawrence or his bitch would be able to get in the house. How dare him to do some bullshit like that in her book. After gaining access to the house, the house was a dirty ass mess. The same wash rag she had left on Monday after having sex with him was still in the same spot. Dishes were all in the sink, clothes all over the den. The place was a mess. All she could say was "Trifling bitches!"

After making fifty and one calls about the kidnapping of Shawn, Lawrence finally answered the call of Pamela. Pamela was some sort of motherly figure in his eyes that she got through to him. She persuaded Lawrence to return Shawn back to Virginia Beach. Leaving dozens of messages on his phone, Lawrence finally called Ebony with the news that he and Shawn were returning back. This was music to her ears. Ebony could hardly sleep. She had not talked to Kim since he had left and she was disappointed that he could leave her in her time of despair.

Since she had changed the locks on the house, she told Lawrence to call her when the two of them got close. About 2 am the call came that they were fifteen minutes out. This was perfect timing, because Ebony only lived about that distance away in Chesapeake.

After meeting up with them at the house, Ebony was more concerned with Shawn's welfare. He was young and didn't know what was going on. Lawrence and Ebony set on the steps and tried to talk over their problems. Lawrence begged Ebony to come back home. She knew that she needed to lay some ground rules down if she were to decide on staying with him. To her, she really could not stand the thought of living in her house where another bitch had laid her head. Ebony didn't feel comfortable with that idea, but knew that they couldn't afford to move elsewhere at the time. She did however state that they could sell the house and move into an apartment until they found another house. Lawrence was hell bent on not moving, he figured that she could just get over the hurt and disgust that was in her mind. They did agree that there would be no more cheating and if things did not work out this time around, they would sell the house, split everything down the middle and go their separate ways.

In the back of Ebony's mind, she wondered how she was gonna tell Kim all that had transpired. After all he did leave her high and dry when she needed him most. Once again looking out for everyone else's feelings, she couldn't think clearly about what she needed. All she knew was that she needed to be with her son, because he needed his mother. Lawrence could not provide the nurturing and affection that a mother could provide for their children.

Kim arrived home around five in the morning, to find his bags packed and at the front door. Ebony tried to explain to him all that had transpired, but to no avail. He didn't want to hear her excuses why she was doing this for her child; he just wanted to get his shit and leave. Her heart was hurting, but she knew she had made the right choice to move home. Shawn really needed her.

Lawrence shelled out two months of rent for Ebony to break her lease. He also paid for a maid service to clean the house before Ebony moved back home. Once there, Ebony got rid of the mattress and box spring. That she could not stomach, knowing another woman was in her home. It seemed like after Lawrence got her back home, all the niceness went out the window.

Chapter 15

Four months had come and gone since she had been back home. It seemed like Lawrence was up to his old tricks again. Ebony had just about had enough. She moved back home for this again! He started calling her bitch everyday and tried to suck the life right out of her. Ebony had moved into the guest bedroom around the fifth month. She knew this time that it was over for good. Forget about her child for the moment, the focus was on her. If her health was not good or if Lawrence tried to kill her, Shawn would be with him anyway.

Ebony just needed to woo-saw and get away. She told Lawrence that she needed a trip; she was going to visit Gwen. He didn't even complain. Ebony packed her bags and headed down the coast. She knew that once she saw her true friend, this would rejuvenate her and bring her back to life. Once she arrived in North Carolina, a sudden calm came over her. The two had to play catch up on things missed since Gwen had been gone. The weekend went by so damn quick. Driving back up the coast, Ebony was dreading returning home.

Lawrence was trying everything to break her, because she had started back to school for her Bachelor's Degree. Most nights just to get peace and quite, she would go over her friend, Diva or Natalie's house and sleep on the floor. Diva, she had met while working at the Police Department. They shared a lot of family values alike. Both of the women liked to cook, do arts and crafts and take care of their sons. Natalie was in Ebony's support group at the women's shelter. Their doors, was always open to Ebony. Often times not to impose on either woman, just so she would not see his face, she would just leave home early in the morning around four o'clock. There really was no place to go that early but Denny's. It seemed that she was there so much in Denny's, every waitress knew her personally. After eating and studying for a while, she would leave about seven. Ebony would go to work and get an hour worth of sleep in the women's bathroom. This became her regular routine.

Ebony didn't know what she was gonna do, but needed to do something. She only found peace and solace at work, but that was also becoming unbearable. Her co-workers had strayed away from her. After all that they had been through together, she couldn't believe that Lawrence had turned them against her also. He called her supervisor and told her that Ebony had tried to kill herself. Ebony and her supervisor were very close and she couldn't understand how she would take his word over hers. Her supervisor sent her to see a psychiatrist. Ebony wasn't crazy, but this motherfucker was trying to make people believe that she was. She went because it was a requirement from the job. After three visits, she was released to fully duty. Ebony just shook her damn head at her supervisor.

Vanessa once again instructed her daughter to come home. She could live rent free in the basement until she got herself together. Ebony was just so bull headed that she was not willing to walk away, unless she had a job there first. Realization finally set in one day that the marriage was over when Lawrence stood at the bottom of the stairs and said, "You know- you are a dumb bitch, for you to be as educated as you are, you are a dumb bitch." At that moment, time stood still and Ebony replied "Yes, I have been a dumb bitch for putting up with your no good ass for ten years. You are absolutely correct."

After Lawrence left out the door, Ebony called Vanessa and told her, she was coming home. She didn't know when, but it would be soon. This was music to her mother's ears. She decided that when the school semester was over, she would move back to Baltimore. Ebony got busy with trying to find a job.

Vanessa told her one day that there was a position at her job for a supervisor. Ebony forwarded her resume to her mother. A couple of days later she received a call stating they wanted her for a job interview. Ebony had to devise a plan on how she was going to go to Baltimore without Lawrence finding out what she was doing. Since Lawrence always eavesdropped on her conversations, Ebony pulled one of his numbers. While talking to her mother, she just said "Yes", "Yes", "Oh really when? I will be there." After hanging up the phone, he wanted to know what was going on. She told him that her mother needed to have a procedure done and that she needed to be there. Being consumed with his other woman; he didn't notice that Ebony had packed two suits in her car.

Ebony arrived in Baltimore and the pieces of the puzzle were finally starting to fall together. Her interview went very well and the job looked promising. Barbara, Vanessa and Ebony went to three different apartment complexes. Even though Vanessa wanted Ebony home with her and Barbara, Ebony needed to do this for herself. They found a complex that Vanessa and Ebony had lived in while she was in high school. She explained to the rental agent her story. The deal was made for a two bedroom. This would be Ebony and Shawn's safe haven away from the abusive situation. The apartment would be waiting for them by the time they arrived.

After returning back to Virginia, Lawrence wanted to know how things went with Vanessa. Ebony lied and stated she is much better. This really wasn't a lie; because Vanessa was finally feeling better that her child was going to be free from this abuser. Five days after returning, she received a call at work. She got the job. All she had to do was get a physical. The director needed to know when she could start. Time was of the essence. Ebony had to finish up the semester first. That would end two weeks into December. It seemed like she left his ass every Christmas. She began to feel glad to get Shawn out of this environment. He deserved so much more.

Ebony didn't know what she said to piss him off. Lawrence threw Ebony's body across the kitchen and began violently choking her. Ebony once again couldn't breath. She had had enough of this shit. Trying to reach for the phone to call the police again, "Call, all I am going to do is lie and get you locked up again", Lawrence taunted. Ebony didn't want to go to jail again, so that was out of the question. This time she finally went to the Naval Hospital. She could barely swallow.

She phone Lawrence and left a message for him to bring Shawn to visit her. He left a voicemail stating, "I hope you die bitch. I ain't bringing him a fucking place." Ebony was running out of options. That same day she went home and held herself hostage in her room. She got the phone book and started calling divorce lawyers. She finally found one that would not charge her an arm and a leg.

The next day she had an appointment and after letting the attorney hear the message, the attorney agreed to do the divorce. Ebony was relieved. This time she wasn't going to fall for his bullshit crying "don't divorce me". She was putting all her faith in God to help her in this situation. Her head came out of the clouds. Since she had wasted Vanessa's money a year ago for a divorce, she convinced Lawrence to pay for at least half. To her surprise, he agreed. This was getting better by the moment, so she thought.

November was ending and it was a month until classes ended. Before attending class one night, Lawrence banged so hard on Ebony's car window; she thought it was going to shatter. He knew she had a test to take that night. She hurried up and pulled out of the driveway as fast as she could to get away from him. Anything could set him off just like that. After arriving in class she was shaken. During the break, she asked the professor could she speak to her in private.

Ebony explained her story to her professor. The professor told her, do not wait any longer. The final requirements for the class, was to turn in a business proposal. All Ebony had to do was complete the final paper and she was guaranteed an A. The quicker she could get this done, the quicker she could get the hell out of dodge.

Ebony got to researching her proposal. She spent numerous of hours in the library on the internet. She had also got her physical results sent to her new employer. Ebony was on her checklist truly. Next she forwarded the rental agent first months rent and the security deposit that was required. Things were starting to fall in place. Tick tock, tick tock.

Everyday that she would come home from work, she would start packing a couple of boxes. Lawrence knew the day was coming that she was leaving, but did not know when. It seemed that Ebony always surprised him. To her, he knew the end was near this time around. Once she ran out of room for storing boxes in her room, she started placing them in the living room. This was a reminder to Lawrence that she was finally going to leave his ass.

The realization didn't really set in for him until he was served with the divorced papers. Without hesitation, he signed them. He had one stipulation before putting his john hancock on the decree though, leave Shawn. At that moment Ebony had to make a choice. Does she stay and fight for her life or will leaving with Shawn break the divorce agreement? In that moment, it was fight or flight. Ebony agreed to leave Shawn.

Things were moving fast. She received a call from her attorney stating that she had a hearing for the divorce. The only thing she needed to bring was a witness to attest to the fact that Lawrence and her did not live as husband and wife for a year. Who on earth could she get to do that? Diva and Natalie was always working. She got the first person at work that was not mad at her, Julie. Julie agreed to go with her for morale support. The two were briefed in the lobby by the attorney of the questions that would be asked. Ebony gave Julie all the correct answers and hoped that she would not forget them. After spending an hour of getting grilled by the Commissioner, Ebony was granted the divorce. The only thing that she agreed to was getting her maiden name back. She did not want any spousal support that she was entitled too, just to be free. Ebony knew that her family had her back and that they would help her get back on her feet.

One week and counting down. Ebony had already given her resignation letter. This was do or die, with no turning back. She had finished her schooling and turned her paper in. Nate had graciously let Ebony use his address for schooling purposes. Now all she needed was someone to help get her clothes out of there. Barbara stepped up and told her granddaughter to find a moving company. Pay the people half of the money and when Ebony made it safely back to Baltimore, she would pay the remaining balance.

The last and final night in Virginia, Ebony needed peace of mind to make this transition. She rented a hotel room and decided to get some much needed sleep. She knew that in order to see Shawn for the last time in a while, she needed to return home before he left for school. Leroy phoned Ebony at four o'clock to give her the details of the weather. The snow was coming down hard in Baltimore and he wanted to make sure she drove careful.

Ebony arose with anxiety in her heart and adrenaline pumping in her veins. Before heading home, she stopped off at the local Wal-mart which was across the street from her house. At 5:30 am the place was empty. She was on a mission to get Shawn his Christmas gift, a mountain bike. She figured that he could grow into it. The salesperson had someone help Ebony get it into her car. She had gassed up already and was ready to get moving once Lawrence left the house. "Get your shit and get the hell out of this town," was all that Ebony could think of.

Apprehension was eating her up inside. But she had to be calm, if she didn't Lawrence would know something was up with her. As she entered the house, the two were upstairs. Ebony politely asked Lawrence to get the bike out of the car and put it away. While he was doing so, she took Shawn in his room. She held him tight and told him that when he came home today, she would be gone. Ebony tried to instill in him that she would always love him, but she had to do this for herself. Since Lawrence always lied, she let Shawn know that she purchased him a bike.

Lawrence and Shawn left the house and Ebony started to work. She started moving all the boxes out of her bedroom downstairs. She was hoping that the moving men would be there within the hour, so they could wrap this up. But to no avail. Ebony was trying to make this process a quick one like the last time. Time was of the essence, but for some reason it wasn't working in her favor this time. She received a call stating that the movers couldn't get there before noon. This was throwing a monkey wrench in her plans. She wanted to be at least half way to Baltimore by then. Ebony had to keep moving. She was tired as hell.

Around two o'clock the movers finally showed up. They had excuse after excuse why they were late. Ebony didn't want to hear shit, she wanted to fucking leave. It seemed like things were moving in slow motion. She started helping move the boxes outside so they can just add them to the truck. Ebony wanted so desperately to take her stereo, but the speakers were mounted to the walls in the family room. It was too many cords to disconnect and she couldn't figure it out. Damn it! "Keep moving girl", she thought to herself. One better she took over two hundred cds. If she was leaving with nothing else, the music was going. This was her passion since a child. Thirty minutes into moving her clothes onto the truck, Lawrence pulled up. "Bitch! What the fuck are you doing?" Everything leading up to getting out of there was coming to a halt. "Damn moving men, for being late," she thought. Lawrence blocked the entrance of the door, so Ebony couldn't get out the house.

AWAKEN by Love

Coming Soon

Words from the Author

Through writing this novel, I learned that the Lord was showing me a different avenue of healing. This has helped heal my soul and I am grateful. I never knew what my purpose in life was, until one day it dawned on me. I had asked the Lord, why go through this struggle with the same man for seventeen years. The outcome was to share my story with you, the reader, so that you could avoid similar situations.

I want women of all races, creed and color to know that you can overcome and be a survivor. When you think you know people, you figure them out wrong. Know deep down in your heart that you can only validate you. You do not need to be validated by any man, or have a man just for validation. God said, "He would be there in your time of need." Deep down in your heart, if you feel that things with your mate are not working out before it gets to the point of the physical, emotional or sexual abuse - leave. It is better to have joy in your heart and peace within your soul. Adhere to your instincts, but also have a Plan B. Remember ladies, you already have a daddy or father that raised you. This is not what a man was placed on this earth for and neither were you. You were placed here to be a virtuous and God fearing woman. Woman was made to help man and to be his companion, not his child, toy, or possession. We, as women, need to hold our heads high and wait for the Lord to send our soul mate to us that will love us unconditionally.

P.S. First we must love ourselves before we can receive and offer love in return.

The woman came from a man's rib. Not from his feet to be walked on. Not from his head to be superior, but from the side to be equal. Under the arm to be protected, and next to the heart to be loved.

Author Unknown.

POWER & CONTROL

USING COERCION & THREATS
- Making her do illegal things
- Making her drop charges
- Making and/or carrying out threats to do something to hurt her
- Threatening to commit suicide/report her to welfare

USING INTIMIDATION
- Making her afraid by using looks, actions, gestures
- Smashing things
- Destroying her property
- Abusing pets
- Displaying weapons

USING EMOTIONAL ABUSE
- Putting her down
- Calling her names
- Making her think she's crazy
- Making her feel bad about herself
- Playing mind games
- Humiliating her
- Making her feel guilty

USING ECONOMIC ABUSE
- Preventing her from getting or keeping a job
- Making her ask for money
- Not letting her know about or have access to the family income
- Taking her money
- Giving her an allowance

USING MALE PRIVILEGE
- Treating her like a servant
- Making all the big decisions
- Acting like the "King of the Castle"
- Being the one to define men's and women's roles

USING CHILDREN
- Making her feel guilty about the children
- Using the children to relay messages
- Using visitation to harass her
- Threatening to take the children away

MINIMIZING, DENYING, BLAMING
- Making light of the abuse and not taking her concerns about it seriously
- saying the abuse didn't happen
- Shifting responsibility for abusive behavior
- Saying she caused it

USING ISOLATION
- Controlling what she does, who she sees, who she talks to, what she reads, where she goes
- Limiting her outside involvement
- Using jealousy to justify actions

PHYSICAL VIOLENCE SEXUAL
PHYSICAL VIOLENCE SEXUAL